"Watch out!"

A black SUV swerved into their path and sped straight toward them. Sheer terror ripped through Talia's heart. Guardrails blurred past in her peripheral vision. She couldn't look away from the hulking SUV in their path.

She screamed again and watched Noah narrow his eyes and adjust his grip. At the last second, he jerked the steering wheel, then righted it again, and they slipped past the vehicle. Talia whipped around to see the SUV squeal on two of its tires as it spun in a one-eighty behind them and continued the chase.

She pounded on the center console. "Go! Go! Go!"

Another look back and the SUV was on their tail. She braced herself for impact, but Noah kept them in their lane as they flew past more cars.

"What do we do?"

"Hang on." His jaw clenched tight.

"What?"

"Hang on to something."

Talia barely had a chance to grab the door handle when her seat belt locked, pinning her to the back of the seat. She squeezed her eyes shut and felt the car brake and spin around...

After growing up on both the east and west coasts, and traveling the world, **Michelle Aleckson** now enjoys living the country life in central Minnesota with her husband and four children. She loves rocking out to '80s tunes on a Saturday night, and playing board games with family and friends. She writes contemporary stories full of romance, grace and, yes, a little sass, too. Connect with her at michellealeckson.com!

Books by Michelle Aleckson

Love Inspired Suspense

Hidden Ranch Peril

Visit the Author Profile page at LoveInspired.com.

HIDDEN RANCH PERIL

MICHELLE ALECKSON

LOVE INSPIRED SUSPENSE
INSPIRATIONAL ROMANCE

LOVE INSPIRED SUSPENSE
INSPIRATIONAL ROMANCE

ISBN-13: 978-1-335-58719-0

Recycling programs
for this product may
not exist in your area.

Hidden Ranch Peril

Love Inspired
22 Adelaide St. West, 41st Floor
Toronto, Ontario M5H 4E3, Canada
www.LoveInspired.com

Printed in U.S.A.

In whom we have redemption through his blood,
the forgiveness of sins, in accordance with
the riches of his grace.
—*Ephesians* 1:7

To my parents, who have always believed in me.
Love you, Mom, Dad & Jan.

ONE

At the sound of a gunshot, Talia Knowles ceased humming and pulled on the reins to keep Peaches from bolting. The palomino's ears pricked up. She pawed the ground but stayed.

One shot could mean anything. Living in the remote Owyhee Mountains meant facing any number of pests where a gun came in handy. Rattlesnakes, rock chucks, coyotes.

A second shot sounded. Guess Aunt Sally wanted her to come in off the trail. Good thing she was on her way back already.

A third shot echoed off the barren rust-colored hills. Talia's breath caught.

Their signal for danger.

Three shots meant run. Run to the neighboring ranch. Talia never questioned the plan when her aunt made it all those years ago, but now all she had were questions. How was she supposed to leave the only family she had left in the world? What danger was she running from? How would her aunt face it alone?

No. She couldn't do it. She couldn't run away without knowing. She wasn't a child anymore. She might be able to help.

"Let's go see what's going on, girl. But we have to be quiet. Aunt Sally will be ticked off that we're not sticking to the plan." Talia nudged the mare's ribs. The saddle creaked as she braced her legs, and they were off. A hard gallop until they reached the crest of the hill. Talia slowed the mare with another tug on the reins and dismounted. Her boots kicked up dust as she skirted the sagebrush and led Peaches to a rock outcropping uphill from the Mustang Sally Ranch house and barns. She yanked her bird-watching binoculars from the saddlebag and crept behind the rocks. The chilly October air whistled through the peaks of stone and sent a shiver down Talia's back despite the thick flannel shirt and puffer vest she wore.

Two unfamiliar black SUVs blocked the long driveway and entrance to the ranch. Way too shiny to be anyone from around here. Those were city vehicles. And two of them? Who had invaded their quiet valley in the Idaho Owyhees?

Aunt Sally stood on the porch in her dusty jeans and barn jacket, that stubborn unreadable face under her old cowgirl hat, and her rifle in her hands. Her voice carried on the wind. "I told you, the girl isn't here. Hasn't been here in years… I don't know where she is."

Were they talking about her? Girl? Talia was almost thirty. Nothing "girly" about that. And why would Sally lie about knowing her? She was the *only* one who really knew her.

Who were these men?

The deeper voice of the man facing away from Talia was impossible to catch.

Sally cocked the gun. "Go on now. She's not here. And I'm not afraid to use this." She pointed it at one of the men. As five others rushed at her, she fired her weapon. One of the men tackled her and wrenched the gun away. She kicked as another grabbed her legs. He flung her over his shoulder. Sally flailed and punched as he dragged her to the second SUV and threw her in.

Sally! Talia had to help her.

She dropped the binoculars, pitched her boot in the stirrups and then froze. How was she supposed to fight off six men?

Aunt Sally wanted her to run to the Jordan Creek Ranch. That's why she fired off the three shots.

Yet how could she leave her?

Her aunt's voice rang in her mind. *No matter what, if you hear those shots, you run. Run to the JC Ranch. Got it?*

Talia grabbed the pommel, hoisted herself up into the saddle, and had the horse moving before her other foot was braced into the stirrup. "Hee-yah. Go, girl!"

As she raced across the desert away from her childhood home, the red hills sped by. Talia leaned farther over the saddle, urging Peaches to go faster. They followed the creek trail. The one she'd just taken for her morning ride to enjoy the clear cerulean sky, the crispness of fall finally in the air with the spicy hint of sage. Now she galloped at a breakneck speed, focused only on the trail and staying in the saddle.

She and Sally had always loved the seclusion out here. But, man, what Talia wouldn't do in this moment for some closer neighbors.

The galloping hoofbeats matched the thundering pulse in her head. Three shots. Run for safety.

But then what?

Help. She needed to get help for Sally.

Wonder if this had anything to do with the weird phone call she received from Aunt Sally yesterday. She said she wanted to talk to Talia about something. Something she didn't want to discuss over the phone. But the late foaling of one of her patients meant Talia didn't get to the ranch until her aunt was in bed last night. And the early morning ride had her out before the sun came up, cell phone left behind, useless as it was with such little reception out here in the wild hills.

After all those years of safety evacuation plans Aunt Sally drilled into her, they were executing Plan Number Twenty-Three. Talia didn't even live on the ranch anymore, having her own cottage in Orchard Springs, an hour away, closer to her practice and most of her patients. But that plan they made so long ago was the only thing holding her together now.

Guess the plans weren't simply a way to make an anxious kid feel secure, but Aunt Sally's way of helping Talia know what to do in certain situations where most people figured it out naturally.

She might not know what to do, but the Polecheski brothers would. She just had to get to their ranch.

Talia gave Peaches another nudge. "Run, girl!"

Both horse and rider were gasping for air by the time Talia jumped from the saddle and ran to the main Jordan Creek barn.

It was quiet, though. Too quiet for a busy horse and cattle ranch in the late morning hours. Where were the brothers? The hands? Anyone?

After the bright sunlight, she couldn't see in the dim barn. Time was running out. "Hello?"

As her eyes adjusted, an unknown yet striking face poked out of the last stall. She strode up to him. He had dark eyes, dark stubble across a strong jaw, a black cowboy hat, and a dirty plaid shirt stretched across broad shoulders. The man leaned on a pitchfork and, now that she got a better look, there was something strangely familiar in his dimpled smile. "Can I help you?"

"Where are Beau and Rob?"

"At an auction. Most of the other hands are with them. Are you okay?"

They weren't here? Talia bent over, hands on her knees, and tried to catch her breath. All that and only some stranger here to help Sally? She stood, hands on her mouth, and paced.

Think. Where was the closest help?

"Ma'am?"

"It's not ma'am. It's Talia. And, yes, I need help." The last word escaped as more of a squeak.

"Talia. Talia Knowles?"

She stopped and looked again. "Yes, I'm Talia Knowles. Who are you?"

"I'm Noah Landers. I've been looking for you for the last seven months."

"Noah Landers? How do you know me?"

Her question resounded through the barn.

Noah scrambled for an answer, but his mind went blank. After all those years of wondering, here she was. Talia Knowles. Although *Talia* was a new name he hadn't heard until yesterday. He had always known her as Anna Coleson.

The age-progression software didn't do her justice. The blonde four-year-old child he remembered as a kid now had curly caramel-colored hair. No more round cheeks or pudgy hands that would tug on his arm and beg for horsey rides. She was a grown woman, tall with an athletic build, and if he wasn't mistaken, she was on the verge of panic. Instead of childlike curiosity, fright was reflected in her big blue eyes.

He still hadn't answered her question about how he knew her. It shouldn't be that hard to explain. But if he did, he'd reveal too much. Sally seemed to think it was better that Talia didn't remember her tragic past, that her whole family was killed in a violent explosion when she was a young child.

He'd have to trust Sally. She was the one who was with Anna—er—Talia all this time. As anxious as he was for answers to his own questions, he promised Sally he would wait.

But how they knew each other didn't matter right now. The woman was scared. Could bolt at any time. And after all the time he'd spent looking for her, he couldn't lose her now.

He took a cautious step toward her, stirring up the scent of fresh hay he'd just laid. He softened his voice, as if trying to calm a spooked mare. "I'm the new ranch hand here. And I, uh, met Sally yesterday. She told me about you. Turns out we knew each other from a long time a—"

"Never mind that. Is anyone else here?" She looked around frantically, chest still heaving as she tried to catch her breath and paced in between the stalls.

"No…"

"Then you'll have to do. You need to help me. Men took her."

"Took who?"

"Sally. They shoved her into some fancy SUV and—"

Noah rushed over and caught Talia by the arm before she collapsed. He led her to a hay bale and helped her sit.

"They, they took her, and I just watched. I ran." She looked up at him. "How could I just run away?"

"Sally? Who took her?"

"I don't know who they are. Six men, two SUVs. She fired the signal to run. And I ran. We have to help her!" She popped up off the bale. "Phone! Where's the phone? We need to call the sheriff."

He followed on her heels as she rushed to the barn office and called 911 on the landline. Her hand shook, but her voice grew steadier as she relayed the information to the dispatcher. Maybe she was calming down.

Who would've taken Sally? And why now, when he was so close to hearing the truth?

Talia hung up the phone. "The sheriff will meet us at the ranch." She marched toward the mare she'd raced in on.

"Wait, you shouldn't ride her so soon. We can take my truck."

She looked back over her shoulder with a frown. "I wasn't going to ride Peaches. I'm a veterinarian. I know how to take care of a horse. I'm going to lead her to the empty stall and give her a quick brush down. It will take at least half an hour for the sheriff to get out here."

"Oh." The woman went from frantic and falling apart to stiff with a businesslike in a matter of minutes. It was a little odd. "Are you sure you're okay?"

"I need to take care of my horse and then get back to Mustang Sally Ranch. Now that I know the sheriff will be here soon, I'm...fine."

He helped her remove the tack and saddle and hurried

to find water for the mare. The traces of panic subsided as Talia crooned in the horse's ear, except for the slight tremor in her hand as she used the curry brush. "We'll find her, Peaches. Don't worry."

She might not be as "fine" as she declared.

Sally's words from last night played through his mind.

You're the spitting image of your dad, Noah. And he saved my life. But I won't trust anyone just yet. So keep quiet about Gregory looking for Talia. I know he's her uncle and he's put out commercials looking for her. Thankfully she doesn't watch TV and hasn't seen them because she's not ready. She was so traumatized that she doesn't remember how her family died. And when I tell her, she'll need time. Time to work through it. I'm afraid of what the shock might do to her.

Looked like time ran out, and now he might never find the answers about his father he was hoping Sally would provide.

Maybe he should just take Talia to her uncle to keep her safe. Gregory Coleson could help them find Sally. The man was wealthy and had plenty of resources.

But Sally was a very convincing woman. That steel grip she had on his arm, the intensity in her eyes when she told him to wait before breaking the news to Talia— well, it wasn't something he could ignore after giving her his word that he would wait.

He would trust that she knew best. For now. But Talia still needed help.

He took the brush from Talia's hand, startled by the warmth that flooded him when their hands touched. "I'll help you. Let's go to Sally's place and wait for the deputies."

She nodded. "Right. And on the way, you can tell me why you look so familiar. I know you from somewhere."

Talia might remember more than Sally realized.

But more importantly, she was in danger. Maybe this was the opportunity to protect her and right some of the wrongs from the past.

TWO

The old red Ford bucked as it hit a pothole in the dirt road. Talia braced her hand against the dash. While she appreciated Noah's urgency, her behind was going to need an ice pack after a morning in the saddle and now this bumpy ride.

And yet, did that really matter? Aunt Sally had been taken.

As they pulled up to the ranch house, Talia was out the door before Noah killed the engine. She stopped a few steps away from the porch.

The same squeak of the windmill, same weathered boards of the porch, same wind chimes sounding on the desert-scented breeze. And yet nothing felt the same without her aunt there.

Looking down, she spied a dark burgundy puddle in the dust at her feet.

Noah squatted next to it. "Blood. Do you know whose it is?"

"Aunt Sally got a shot off before the men overpowered her. She must've hit one of them."

What was going on that would bring bloodshed to their ranch?

Talia stepped around it and entered the house. The lingering scent of coffee and bacon in the air turned her stomach. Had she come home from her ride on a normal morning and walked into such a smell, her stomach would be grumbling with gratitude. Now it was a haunting question. Was that Aunt Sally's last meal?

Noah gently guided her to one of the dining room chairs. "You okay?"

"No. But that's not important right now."

Talia took stock of the room. The dining room table wasn't clear like she left it this morning. Now it was littered with papers, a notebook and pen, Sally's laptop, and a dusty box labeled Talia's Toys. She stood and rifled through some of her old horse figurine collection and favorite childhood books all jumbled in the box and a few trinkets scattered on the table. Why would Sally have this out? Talia wasn't even sure why Sally had kept this stuff. Sally always said she saved it for Talia's future children, but that wasn't gonna happen no matter how much she longed for a family of her own.

She was always on the outside looking in. Aunt Sally said she saw the world differently and that it was a gift. But she learned from Danny she didn't have what it took to connect emotionally with other humans. Not on the level required for marriage. And she had come to terms with it. There was plenty good she could do with her mustangs and her patients. She was useful. She just wouldn't be able to continue her own family line.

"Look at this." Noah's voice pulled her out of her regrets. He was looking at the laptop screen, but Sally's familiar scribble on the notebook drew her attention. "Key = mustang."

"What does that mean?"

"I don't know, but did Sally mention taking a trip to Seattle?"

"No. Why?"

"She was browsing airline tickets for two to Seattle."

Seattle? That part of their lives was so long ago. Why would she go back?

A siren pierced the morning stillness, interrupting her thoughts.

Talia and Noah met the sheriff and the deputy in the driveway. The sheriff looked just like his campaign picture, silvery-gray hair, bushy mustache, brawny. The other guy could've been blown away by the wind, he was so lanky. But he was studying their surroundings, alert. Probably made him a good cop.

The older man removed his hat as he approached them. "I'm Sheriff Daniels, and this is Deputy Wells. I understand there was an abduction?"

"Yes." Talia told the sheriff what she had seen, purposeful to keep emotion out of her report and stick to facts. She answered Sheriff Daniels's questions while Wells did a careful search around the house.

When she finished, Sheriff Daniels turned to Noah. "And how about you? Did you see anything?"

Before Noah could say a word, Talia stepped forward. "I told you, he wasn't even here when it happened."

"Hang tight there, ma'am. I understand. But I want to hear what he has to say."

Talia clenched her jaw tight. Such a waste of time. They should be out looking for Sally.

The sheriff jotted something down in his notepad. "And how do you know the women here?"

"Oh, I, uh—"

"Like I told you, Sheriff, Noah wasn't here. I already

answered that question twice. I met him at the neighbors' ranch. He was the only one there and offered me a ride. Now, what do we need to do next to find Sally? Every minute you waste here, the farther away she is."

He closed his notepad and slipped it into his pocket. "Deputy Wells is calling this in, and we've got everyone in the county on the lookout for those SUVs. But the more information we have, the better prepared we are. As for finding Sally, the best thing you can do is stay put and stay out of the way. Sounds like they were looking for you if they asked about a girl. Maybe you should come with us to the station. They may come back for you."

"I'm not going to sit in some office and wait. I can help."

"Look, if they find you, then we'll be spreading ourselves even thinner. If you won't come with us, it's better if you stay off the grid and out of the way. I can't force you, but I'll say it again, I think you should come so we can keep you safe."

Talia shook her head. "No. I can take care of myself. Besides, I have patients that need me."

The sheriff's mustached twitched as he frowned.

Noah spoke up. "I'll stay with Talia and help keep her safe."

"And how you do you propose you'll do that?"

"I'm a former marine. I have a couple tours under my belt. I have a permit to carry a firearm."

"Fine, but at least stay out of the way of the investigation." Sheriff Daniels turned to Talia. "If you want to help, write a list of anybody you can think of that might have a reason to kidnap Sally or come after you."

Not sure how that was a big help. Nobody came to

mind. "And you'll let us know as soon as you find anything?"

"Just stay put and let us do our job. I'll contact you when we find her." He called to Wells. "You get that blood sample?"

Wells nodded. They did a sweep of the driveway and turned toward the barn.

Yeah, that whole staying put thing wasn't going to happen. But once these guys left, maybe she could do her own investigating. And if Noah was handy with a gun, maybe she'd keep him around too. Besides, she still needed to figure out why his face brought back shadows of happy memories. Nothing clear, no pictures or sounds that she could recall, just a vague sense of familiarity kept coming to mind every time she looked at him.

She studied his tanned face under the black Stetson. Warm brown eyes with small wrinkles in the corners that made him look like he was always smirking and a dimple in his left cheek.

As she cataloged Noah's handsome features, something bubbled inside, like a slow flow of hot fudge over ice cream, something sweet and captivating.

Whatever that was would have to be considered later. No room in her life for romance. No time to worry about something so frivolous when Sally was in danger.

As soon as the sheriff and deputy left, Talia turned to her newly appointed protector. "I'm not going to sit and wait for news. If you want to stick around and help, great. But if not, I won't hold it against you."

Noah pushed off from the porch beam he'd been leaning on. "I'm a man of my word, Talia. I'll keep you safe."

She studied him again. He certainly looked sincere. But she'd been fooled before when she thought people cared about her only to find herself a source of entertainment when she became the butt of their jokes. She was far too gullible in her younger years.

Should she trust him?

She'd have to risk it. She would need someone to watch her back if those men were really looking for her. Sally was as tough as they came, and they took her down in a flash.

"Alright. Then let's go back to my place in Orchard Springs. Looks like Sally was going through some of my old toys looking for something. I have two more boxes at my house."

"Do you think she's looking for a key? Like she wrote in that notebook?"

Key = mustang.

Talia shrugged. "I don't know. But it's somewhere to start."

Noah leaned against his faithful red Ford in the driveway of Mustang Sally Ranch, letting the cool air with the familiar scent of horses and dust ground him. Good thing Talia ran inside to grab her phone and things. He was still reeling.

After all those years, here she was. Seeing Anna— no, Talia—standing there on the porch earlier telling the sheriff what happened, a flood of memories and emotions hit him. Thankfully the soldier in him knew how to compartmentalize and tuck the grief from their tragic past away. A past she didn't even remember.

And what made him volunteer to protect her? He still heard screams in his sleep, swore he could smell the smoke and blood from the last time he was protecting a woman.

Maybe this was his chance at redemption. A chance to put those memories to rest for good.

For now, he would have to put his original plans on hold and help Talia. Yeah, he hoped Sally would tell him about that night she and Talia disappeared, about how his father died. Was he a hero or a traitor? What kind of blood ran through Noah's veins? After the fiasco in Afghanistan, he wasn't sure who he was anymore.

But he'd promised Sally he would wait to tell Talia about her uncle. And now it looked like Talia was in danger. He'd have to help her find Sally first and worry about finding the secrets of his past later.

Not that he would begrudge the chance to get to know the woman walking toward him with a fierceness in her blue eyes that told of her loyalty to Sally. But it would be a balancing act of waiting to tell her about her family and trying to build trust.

"You ready?"

Her voice cut through his musings.

"Yeah. Let's go."

They hopped in his truck and headed north toward Orchard Springs.

As soon as they pulled out of the driveway, she folded her arms across her chest and stared at him. "So, Noah Landers. How do you know me? And be more specific this time."

Great. The question he'd been dreading to answer. "You don't waste any time, do you?" He grinned, trying to brush off the question.

One glance and she quirked an eyebrow up. "No, I don't. Answer the question."

How much did he share? How much did she know? Sally said Talia didn't have any memories of her earliest years. She deserved to know something, but he had to keep his word to Sally too.

Speak the truth. Keep it safe. "I…was your brother's friend."

She gasped. Even with his eyes on the road, he could feel her weighty stare.

"My…my brother?"

"Yeah, Alexander. We were best friends."

"Xander?"

He glanced over, catching the shock on her face. "You remember?"

"Not really. I… I don't have many memories of my family before they were killed. Sally always kept information about them vague. But the name just came to me." She leaned closer to him. "You were Xander's best friend. And you were looking for me?"

He always prided himself on being a man of his word. But how did he keep his word to Sally and yet tell Talia the truth? She didn't want Talia to know about Gregory yet, but he was the reason he had the means to come looking for her. Gregory promised he'd help look after Noah's mom and the ranch if Noah could find his niece. Coleson's generous offer for their stud services with Excalibur, put them in the black for the year and gave them enough of a cushion that Noah could take the time to look for Talia and Sally.

Noah glanced over at Talia in the passenger seat. Eagerness for more was so evident on her face. But he didn't want to upset her. "I know we were only kids when everything happened. Xander and I were nine when he died and you…left, but I always wondered about you, where you'd end up. I had some time and wanted to see this part of the country. I hoped to find you but wasn't sure I could. Thought I'd ask around as I traveled."

"How *did* you find us?"

"Caro—" He cleared his throat. "Sally's stories."

"What did you call her?"

Oh no. She didn't even know about the name change? "Um, I knew her as Carol. And your name was Anna. Do you remember any of that?"

"No. But it sounds familiar." Talia turned to the window, a stiffness to her shoulder. "Carol," she whispered. "Anna." Her breath fogged up the passenger window. "Why would she change our names?"

He kept his lips still. She didn't demand an answer. Instead, the whir of the tires beneath them rumbling down the country road was the only noise for minutes. It was a tense silence. He could almost feel her mind working through the information he gave her. Three names.

Sally was right. Talia had a lot to process. And that wasn't even a big part of her secret past. The best thing he could do was let her come to terms with it. A new name was something one didn't take lightly. He knew.

His own memories took over. Memories of playing with Xander, hanging out at the Coleson mansion, swimming in the Olympic-size pool, making forts, and all the things little boys loved to do. And the Colesons never made Noah feel different because his father worked for them as the head of their security. They always treated him like one of the family. He never minded Anna tagging along with them. She was a serious child. Quiet around many, but she loved bossing Noah around. Guess she hadn't outgrown any of that.

"Why did she change our names?" her voice cut through the memories.

"I'm not sure why." Which was true. He was only a kid when Carol and Anna disappeared. How would he know?

"What stories led you to us?"

Finally, something he could answer. "Stories about the mustangs in the Owyhee Mountains. Even though we lived in the city back then, San Jose, you loved horses. Our families would spend weekends at my grandpa's ranch up in the Sierra Nevadas. Every night you would ask for another story about the mustangs. Carol always obliged. Even though Xander and I wouldn't admit it, we always liked those stories too."

"So stories led you to us?"

"They were some of the happiest memories we had together, before you lost your family, so I wondered if you'd end up there."

"What about your job? You left everything to come searching for us?"

"Truth is, I needed a break. My last tour in Afghanistan, I lost someone I was supposed to be protecting and it…well, it shook me. I came back to Landers Ranch and my family, but I needed to get away for a while. I had this time to travel through the area and signed on at the big horse ranches as a hand. Started down in Nevada and worked my way north through the Owyhees, keeping an eye out for you or Carol. And any wild mustangs I could find, of course."

Her delicate brows knitted as she worked another piece of the puzzle. He forced a charming smile even as his breath caught. Had he gone too far? She had to trust him. So much was riding on it.

"Why do you think those men took Sally? Why are they looking for me?"

Noah blew out a hard breath, thumb drumming against the cracked vinyl steering wheel. "I don't know." And that worried him. He'd feel a lot better if he could take Talia straight to her uncle. But Sally was so insistent.

"Well, whoever they are, we need to find Sally. She's the only family I have left. I can't lose her too."

"I know. I'll do whatever I can to help you."

"Why?"

He glanced over at her. "What do you mean?"

"Why are you willing to put yourself in danger to protect me and look for Sally?"

He stared at the barely-there line in the middle of the road. The question struck him to the core. But how much of his reason could he share? "Sally knew my dad. He's gone now, but I wanted to talk to her about him."

"How'd he die?"

Wow. Most people tiptoed around and avoided that question like it was a rabid skunk. She barreled on in and asked anyway.

The desert brush blurred as they sped past. He took a few deep breaths to push back the burning in his throat. *Keep it vague.*

"He died in an explosion."

"I see." Her voice dropped low. "I guess we share more than just a history."

"What's that?"

"We both lost our fathers."

All he could give her was a curt nod.

Of course, he lost his father at the same time she lost both parents, a brother and two sisters. But that same instant changed their paths irrevocably. And then she disappeared.

He owed her so much.

His father failed to protect them. Not only did he fail, many blamed Henry Dillard. Said he helped the East Fourteenth Street gang plant the bombs in the mansion that killed the Colesons.

Noah didn't know who to believe. His mom, who hailed his father a hero, dying to protect the family they all loved, or the media, who called his death poetic justice when he got caught in the blast meant for his employers.

Finding Sally and Talia was supposed to clear that up.

After years of wondering what happened that night, he was so close to knowing the truth.

He found Sally yesterday. She came to the Jordan Creek Ranch to return a trailer she'd borrowed. He recognized her immediately. He knew she recognized him too. The moment their eyes locked, she paled. But the busy ranch was no place to talk. Thus they arranged a time today to visit, and she left him with the admonition to keep Talia's past quiet for now.

Just when he was so close to answers, she was gone.

"I don't want you to lose anyone else you care about, Talia. I know what it's like. And our families were really close at one point. My father was head of security for your family, and also your father's best man at his wedding. They aren't here to protect you anymore, but I am. I'm here to help you find Sally and to keep you both safe."

"Thank you."

He tried to smile. Would she still say that when she knew the whole truth?

Probably not.

THREE

Once they approached the Treasure Valley, Talia traced the winding Snake River below them. The morning sun she had enjoyed on her early ride was now replaced with ominous clouds. No twinkling light reflected off the water as it usually did. Instead, the river looked dark and murky as it cut through her town in the distance.

Never had the body of water reminded her of its name as it did now. And as much as she loved animals, she'd never been fond of snakes.

They passed the Orchard Springs city limit sign. The small town proved itself a good place for an introverted veterinarian to live. Neighbors were much closer than out at the ranch, but most kept to themselves. The necessary interactions with them were short and sweet when needed. Talia had even been over to a few of their homes for small gatherings.

She'd come a long way since childhood.

But right now, she needed to find her aunt. "Turn left here. That's my place, second on the right." The moment Noah pulled into the driveway of her white-sided cottage with the blue door, her anxiety dipped down a notch, helping ease the breath that never quite felt deep enough since she watched strangers stuff her aunt into a car and speed off.

Noah craned his neck, checking all around as he got out of the truck and followed her to the porch. "What are we looking for here again?"

She slipped her key into the lock. "Since Sally was going through my childhood things, I have a couple of boxes here we can check. If she was looking for a key or a mustang, I might have it here. I also have a lot of research on mustangs in the different Bureau of Land Management programs. I want to go through my notes."

She led the way through her living room.

Noah spun around in a slow circle. "You must be a minimalist."

"Why do you say that?"

"There's not one picture on the walls or fruity-smelling candle to be seen. Or bowls filled with weird balls of twine and twigs like my mom and sister have. I thought girls liked to decorate their homes with all that stuff."

She glanced at the stark tan walls and oak floors. She had a rug at least. A plain gray rug that served its purpose to protect the flooring from the leather love seat and couch. What else did she need? She turned down the short hall to the front bedroom she used for a home office. "If you haven't figured it out by now, I'm not like most women. I have what I need. And I spend a lot of free time at the ranch helping Sally."

"So why don't you live there?"

"I love it out there, but it just didn't make sense to locate my practice there. I'm more centralized here and accessible to patients."

His voice from the hall followed her. "Please tell me you have a TV somewhere."

"Why should I when I don't have time for it? I do watch the occasional documentary on my laptop."

Bypassing the sparse desk, she headed straight to the closet and pulled down two small boxes, one a shoe box that her favorite pair of cowgirl boots arrived in, the other a smaller plastic container. She plopped them down on the desk and opened the container.

Noah moved from the doorway and stood next to her. "That's all your childhood stuff? Where are all your third-grade book reports or high school yearbooks?"

She shrugged. "There weren't many memories from childhood I wanted to keep. We moved around so much, and I struggled emotionally in school. I think Sally kept moving us hoping we would find a place I could fit in."

"Did you?"

"Not really. I didn't have many friends. At least, not human ones."

"Animals were always more interesting to you."

"Of course. They were always easier to understand. Human socialization is something I've never mastered. Animals are much more straightforward."

"So you became a vet?" He pointed to her degree hanging on the wall.

"Yes. I started my practice a few years ago. I special-ize in equestrian care."

"No surprise there." He smiled at her, and that hot fudge feeling swirled through her again.

Sally. She needed a clue to find Sally.

Trying to ignore Noah, Talia laid a worn copy of *Black Beauty*, more plastic horses she had collected, and a pile of ribbons from school science fairs out on the desk. Plunging her hand to the bottom of the boot box, she touched something soft with her fingers. She pulled out a stuffed animal, a horse, rusty brown with a white star on the forehead and a braided tail. "Sunny!"

She held her old friend up to her nose and breathed deep. She still smelled slightly of campfire smoke and the floral fabric softener Sally always used. How had she forgotten the old girl? The faithful companion of her childhood she couldn't bear to get rid of. And while many memories of her past weren't easy to relive, this fuzzy friend brought back an aching sense of nostalgia.

"Are you going to introduce me?"

Her spine stiffened.

Noah watched her. He probably thought she was odd, hugging an old stuffed animal like a toddler.

He took Sunny's hoof between two fingers and shook it as he bowed. "Noah Landers at your service."

That was all he had to say? No mean jokes? No teasing?

His head quirked to the side. "You are going to introduce me, right?"

Oh. He was serious.

"Uh, this is Sunny."

"I think we've met before. Didn't you get her for your fourth birthday?"

"Did I?"

He nodded. "If it's the same horse, I helped Xander pick it out for you. It's a little hard to tell since it's been so loved. But I'm pretty sure it is. We had to go to five different stores to get the right one, with the white star on the forehead."

She stared down at the glossy black eyes, fingers trailing the braided mane. Had she really had Sunny that long? A gift from her brother? How had she forgotten so much?

Maybe that's why she could never toss the toy in the giveaway box. She actually held something from her time with her family.

If only she could remember them.

A loud popping sound came from the front of the house.

"Get down!" Noah pulled her to the carpet and covered her with his body.

The sounds didn't stop. "What...what is that?"

He spoke right into her ear. "Gunshots. They're coming from the front of the house. Come on! Keep your head down!"

They crawled to the hallway. Windows shattered in the office behind them and in the living area. Shots fired over them. Noah pushed her across the hall and into her bedroom. She ducked behind her dresser as he slammed the door shut. He rushed to her window overlooking the backyard and peered through the blinds. "I don't see anyone in the backyard. We'll need to get out this way and make a run for the house behind you. Okay?"

All she could do was nod.

He stood and yanked on the old wooden window frame.

It didn't budge.

"When's the last time you opened this thing?" His voice strained as he pushed against the frame.

"Never. I haven't been able to open that one, and I was saving up to have all the windows replaced."

A crash from the entry. They were coming!

Noah dragged the dresser in front of the closed door. Back at the window, he yanked the blinds down off the frame. "You're gonna have to replace this one sooner than you might've expected. Stand back." He took the small lamp base by her bedside table and pitched it through the glass, then wrapped her throw blanket around his hand and cleared the shards still framing the opening.

More crashes sounded from the front of the house.

"Come on!" He grabbed her hand and shoved her through the small window. She landed, twisting her ankle a little, still holding Sunny in her hand. She looked up to see Noah trying to fit his broad shoulders through. He landed next to her with a thud, took her hand and dashed across the small backyard to the cedar fence. He hoisted her up and over.

She landed in the neighbor's rosebushes as more bullets flew over her head.

Noah hopped over. "You okay?"

Was she? She was shaking all over, scratched by thorns and had a throbbing ankle.

But she was alive. "I'm okay."

"Good. We need a vehicle. We've got to get out of here."

Vehicle. Vehicle. How could they…wait! "My neighbors are in Arizona for next six months. We can take their car."

"Let's go. And hurry!"

She bolted along the side of the trailer house to the street. Two houses down, across the street from the river, she spied the Alonzos' empty home. She pointed. "There."

They sprinted to the garage. With shaking fingers, she punched the code into the keypad—the code they'd given her to enter the house and check on their plants.

She let them in the small side door and found the car keys hanging on the hook where Karri said they would be in case of emergency. The Honda crossover engine roared to life as she started the car.

Noah grabbed a towel from a stack on a shelf and hopped into the passenger seat.

She smashed the button to open the garage door and squealed out onto 2nd Avenue. "Should we try to follow these guys and see if they lead us to Sally?"

"No. There's too many of them. We need to outrun them. Just go!"

She ignored the pain in her ankle as she pressed hard on the gas and made a quick right. She wove through the small town and floored it until they made it to the highway.

She checked the mirror. "Now where? Are you sure we shouldn't try to follow them?"

"No, as we turned, one of them ran out into the street. They saw this car and will be looking for it. We need a safe place to hide." He laid his head back on the car rest. "Besides, I could use some doctoring."

What?

She glanced over. His hand was clamped with the towel over his bicep. Blood oozed between his fingers and stained the cloth.

He was hit.

Talia sped down Interstate 84 while Noah tried to keep blood off the leather seats of the car they'd stolen.

How was it he made it through two tours in Afghanistan without any physical scars, and now trying to undo all the damage his father did so long ago cost him a bullet?

Either way, his arm was on fire, like someone dropped red-hot lava into his bicep. A low grunt escaped.

Talia frowned as she glanced at him. "Keep pressure on it."

"I am."

He didn't mean to be rude, but could the woman not see he had a vise grip on the wound?

"Is it a through and through?"

He had already checked. "No. Gonna need you to remove the bullet, Doc."

She swerved hard, almost going off the road. "What? Me? I work with horses. Not humans!"

"Too bad. I left a blood trail. They know one of us is hit, and if they're smart, the first thing they'll do is check hospitals and clinics. And if they found your house, they know where your practice is too. So that's out of the question."

Her voice pitched higher, almost a squeak. "I don't have any equipment. Meds. Tools. How am I supposed to do a surgical procedure in a nonsterile environment? That's begging for an infection."

"Do you think it's better to keep the bullet in my arm?"

She kept her eyes on the road, but her forehead wrinkled, and her lips thinned. Guess she took even a rhetorical question seriously. If he hadn't been in so much pain, he would have laughed.

She glanced over at him and blew out a short breath. "You're right. We need to remove the bullet. But where am I supposed to do that? Or get the supplies I need?"

"Where do you get the stuff for your office?"

"It's all ordered online and delivered."

"Pharmacy?"

"There's no surgical aisle there, Noah." She glared at him for a split second.

Oh, that look took him back. There was that stubbornness. Good. Judging by her reaction, she would need every bit of it to get through this. "Talia, you're gonna have to improvise."

In the silence between them, raindrops started splattering on the windshield. She exited in the next town and parked in a restaurant parking lot right off the ramp. She turned to him. Her voice shook. "Look, I'm a good veterinarian, but I'm not an improviser. It's a stretch for me to think about working on a human body. I can't do this without a sterile room."

The blood seeped through the towel and dripped bright red onto the beige seat. Great. Another mess he'd have to clean up.

He didn't have time for this. He clenched his jaw and closed his eyes, trying to breathe through the pain. "So, find one."

When he opened his eyes, she was doing that thing again where she stared over his shoulder, tapping her fingers against her leg. Her thinking face.

She was oblivious to him studying her. Her pretty face a momentary distraction from the searing pain. Her striking blue eyes held sparks of green, and the smattering of freckles across her pert nose gave a hint of the little girl he used to know. She had no makeup on whatsoever, no jewelry, curly hair pulled back in a low no-nonsense ponytail. But, man, she was gorgeous.

He should probably push that thought aside, send it deep to the recesses of his mind and never let it surface again. He would never have any kind of future with Talia.

Like his father, he failed to protect the ones entrusted to his care. If he had done his job right in Afghanistan, Kelley would still be alive.

But no. She died from a bullet he should've shielded her from.

He might have changed his last name to his mother's maiden name, Landers, but Dillard blood still flowed through his veins, and Dillard men had a way of messing up in the worst possible way. He'd thought going into the marines would make him a better protector, but apparently not.

Talia would soon know of his past. And how could she overlook the dishonor of the Dillard name?

She grabbed his arm. He bit back a roar.

"I might have a place."

"Okay. Can you let go of my arm?" he asked through gritted teeth.

"Oh. Sorry." She looked down at her hand, now covered with blood.

"Here. Wipe it on my jeans and let's get to wherever we're going before I pass out from blood loss."

"Right. It's not far." She wiped her hand on the leg of his jeans.

He cleared his throat. "So...so where are you taking me?"

She bit her lip and cranked the wheel to maneuver back to the main road. The loud diesel engine of semi-truck passing them drowned out all other sounds.

"Talia?"

"Yeah?"

"Where are we going?"

"To my fiancé's."

FOUR

Talia drove through the wet streets. Usually the swish of the windshield wipers helped steady her nerves.

Not today.

Danny was not going to like this.

But it was up to her to get that bullet out of Noah's arm, and Danny's operating room at the animal hospital was the only place she could do it safely.

Hopefully, he would see past their issues and understand the urgency. He had to. This was their only option.

She made another turn and parked next to Danny's green pickup truck behind the hospital. Since there was only one car in the front parking lot, he probably didn't have many patients. She sent up a quick prayer that the operating room was free.

"We're here."

Noah, his face pale, smiled weakly as he looked over at her. "Knew you'd figure something out."

A bubbly feeling inside made her pulse jump and quieted the unease. He believed in her.

And he was right. She did figure something out. She improvised. Kinda.

But enough of that. She found a place. Now she actually had to do surgery. On a human.

They dodged raindrops, and Noah leaned against the wet brick wall while she knocked on the back door of the animal hospital.

Nothing.

Rain ran down her back, soaking her vest. *Come on, Danny.*

She studied her patient. Noah's clenched jaw, shallow breaths as he seemed to push through the pain, the rain running off his hat. Poor guy need help now.

Forget the knocking. Talia pounded on the metal door and yelled. "Danny, it's Talia. Let us in!"

Another minute passed. Her fist started to throb when the doorknob squeaked, and Danny opened up.

"Talia? What are you doi—"

"Sorry, we don't have time to explain." She tugged on Noah's good arm and pushed him through the doorway into the hall. "We need your operating room."

"What? Who is this guy, and why do want to commandeer my OR?"

"Danny, you'll just have to trust me on this. Noah was shot. I need to get the bullet out."

"Shot? That's what emergency rooms are for! You're not a medical doctor!"

"Believe me, I know." She didn't have time for this. She led Noah to the animal operating room.

Danny sputtered behind them as she sat Noah on the table and started scanning the different drugs in the locked cabinet. "You can't do this, Talia. We could lose our licenses!"

She opened a drawer and pulled out a surgical kit, rifled through more cabinets. Where did he keep the sutures? "Fine. Don't help. Tell them we held you against your will." She stopped and looked directly at Danny. "But think about it. Would I do this if there were any other options?"

They stared at each other a beat. He shook his head and rolled his eyes. "You never do anything without a good reason, so I guess not. But do you even know what you're doing?"

"I'll give him a local, remove the bullet, cleanse and close up the wound. Oh, and I'll need to give him some antibiotics."

"Yeah, but…" He pinched his nose. "Forget it. I know I'll never be able to change your mind. I've learned that the hard way." He pushed his hair off his forehead and fisted his hands on his hips. "But I can't be a part of this, so I'm stepping out. And if anyone asks, I never knew you were here. I won't risk my career."

He dropped his keys to the locked cabinets onto the counter and stormed out of the room, the door slamming shut behind him. Didn't take a genius to know he was ticked. She'd have to deal with that later.

Noah whistled. "Nice guy."

"Usually he is. He's just very protective of his practice. He's invested a lot in it."

"So, when's your big day?"

"What big day?" She took Danny's keys and pulled out the anesthetic and the antibiotics she would need from the locked cabinet.

"*The* big day. The wedding? This is the guy you're going to marry, right?"

Talia dropped the box of pills on the counter and whipped her head to look at Noah. "Marry him?" Yeah, at one point she thought Danny was the answer to making her feel normal. But no.

"Yeah. You said he was your fiancé in the car."

"You must not have heard me correctly. He's my *ex*-fiancé."

Noah for some reason looked a little more relaxed. "Oh." He pulled the bloody towel off his arm. "Okay, then, if you don't mind, I'm ready to get this bullet out."

"Right." Talia laid out a few pads on the table and a sterile sheet. "Lay down and try to relax while I scrub up."

She stepped out of the room to the sink. The familiar smell of the antimicrobial soap in the iodine hand brush and motions of scrubbing helped settle her hands. A simple bullet extraction. She could do this. At least she found a clean place. Less risk of infection. Danny always followed strict sterilization procedures.

Looking through the window, she could see Noah lying under the blinding lights of the surgical room. He had removed his hat. His dark hair curling on the white linens, his tan face now almost as pale as the sheet under him. Blood dripping down his arm. He shifted on the table and grimaced. He needed her now.

With a nod of determination for her own benefit, she donned the surgical gown and gloves and entered the room. It wasn't a perfect scrub-in procedure without techs helping, but she could do this.

Noah turned as she came in. "'Bout time, Doc. I thought you were gonna leave me here to bleed out."

She stopped mid-stride. Her horror at such a thought pinched her vocal cords. "I would never do that. I wouldn't leave a patient in trouble."

He chuckled. "Easy now, Talia. I was joking."

"Oh." She set up her kit and tools on the tray, grateful for the mask that hid the heat of her blushing cheeks.

Jokes. Stupid things. So hard to detect. There was nothing funny about surgery or letting a patient bleed out. Even a human one.

"Talia?"

"What?"

"Hey, relax those brows. You've got them knotted up so tight they might snap."

She tried to relax her forehead.

Noah smiled. "You know, Xander used to do the same thing when he couldn't work out a math problem, and I would joke around to help him. I didn't mean to upset you. Only trying to lighten the mood. And maybe the pain is getting to me a little."

"Well, for the record, I'm not great at detecting sarcasm or humor. Sally always said I take things too literally. But I just don't think there's anything humorous about being incompetent or letting a patient suffer inhumanely."

"Sorry." He paused. "I should've remembered."

"Remember what?"

"Xander and I used to rile you up when we wanted you to stop following us. It didn't take much."

"Xander didn't like me following him around?"

"Don't get me wrong. Your brother thought the world of you. But sometimes a nine-year-old boy wanted to do something without his little sister tattling."

It made sense. Five years' difference at that age, not many brothers would tolerate a nagging preschooler. But something inside confirmed what Noah said. Xander loved her. If only she could've had more time with him to make her own memories before that fateful car accident almost twenty-six years ago.

With a fortifying breath, she got back to the task at hand. "I guess I should get that bullet out of your arm."

She cut off Noah's plaid shirt, washed out the wound, and administered a local anesthetic. After scrubbing his skin with the chlorhexidine, she opened the surgical kit.

She just had to pretend Noah was a horse and she'd be fine. "Alright. I need you stay extremely still." Within minutes she dropped the slug into the metal dish. *Plink.* "Got the bullet. Now I'll clean this out and sew you back up."

"Appreciate that, Doc."

A few minutes later, she snipped the last suture. "Done. Now we just need to—"

Danny rushed in. "I don't know what you are tangled up in, but some pretty mean-looking guys just squealed into the parking lot. You better get out of here. Now."

Noah bolted off the table and swayed.

Talia helped prop him up. "Take it easy."

"We don't have time. Let's go!"

She grabbed a box of antibiotics off the counter while Noah reached for his hat and gun. They ran down the hall and out the back, this time the rain pouring down as they raced for the car.

Noah fumbled for the door handle, slick with rain. He fell into the front seat while Talia started the car. These guys must've really done their homework. It wouldn't be hard to track her down to the nearest vet clinic, especially with the fiancé connection.

Fiancé. No, make that ex-fiancé.

It still shook him for some reason that she almost

married that Danny character. Reasons he didn't have time to contemplate.

One of the men rushed around the building and headed straight for them, his black trench coat flying behind him like a dark cape. He pulled the gun from his holster as Talia whipped the car around and raced out of the parking lot.

Noah braced his feet, as if he could make the vehicle go faster by pressing down on an invisible gas pedal. "Go, go, go!"

"Where?"

He spun to look behind them. Their bad guy hopped into a gray sedan and was soon on their tail. "I don't know, but make it fast."

Their tires squealed as they sped through a residential area. Talia must know the area somewhat as she made fast turns and raced down an alley. Another turn and they were back on a main street, mingling with the afternoon traffic. No sign of the gray sedan for the moment.

Noah opened a map on his phone. "We have to get out of here. We can't go back to your place, or the ranch."

"I think I know where we can go. One of my clients has a cabin up in the Sawtooth Range. It's a few hours away. They mostly use it in the summer for trail rides. I made an emergency trip once to treat their horses. They said I could use it anytime."

"Can it be tracked back to you?"

"I don't think so. I have a lot of patients, and I've never taken them up on their offer before."

"It's worth a shot. Head there. The faster the better." He watched behind them as she made her way to the foothills.

After ten minutes without a sign of their tail, Noah

slumped back in the passenger seat and sighed. He didn't want to worry her, but the adrenaline and the local anesthetic she'd given him were wearing off. The dizziness was getting to him. If they could find a place where they could lie low, he could crash for an hour or two and hopefully find some painkillers.

Some protector he was.

Talia handed him her phone. "We should call Sheriff Daniels now. We'll lose reception soon."

"On it." At least he was useful for something. He called the sheriff on speakerphone and told him of the shoot-out at Talia's home and the one they dodged at the animal hospital.

The good sheriff wasn't happy. "This is serious now. You two should head to the nearest police station and stay put."

Talia shook her head. "No. We'll be safe at the cabin. Only my clients know where it is. Have you found Sally?"

"Took a sample of the blood from the ranch, and a few other clues, but it will take the lab a while to process those. No other word on where they might've taken her. Got BOLOs out on the vehicles but nothing yet. Now, wherever you are, you need to find protect—"

The call cut out.

Protection. Right. But these thugs already tracked Talia's house down. Her office building was probably being watched too. Noah didn't know anybody in the area. This cabin was their best bet.

Noah took his hat off and laid his head back on the seat, letting another wave of nausea pass. Without reception, he couldn't waste his phone battery. He turned his phone off and then Talia's.

With a hazy mind, he tried to sort out what they knew. What the next step should be. These guys were serious. They took Sally. They shot up Talia's house. In the middle of the day, in a small town. They couldn't be too professional, since they didn't think to cover the backyard or any of the exits. But they were smart enough to track them down to the vet hospital. Were they just trying to scare them?

Looking down at the bullet hole in his arm, probably not. They were out to kill. But why?

No answers came.

An hour later, Talia pulled into a gas station. "We'll need some water and supplies. I'll be back in a few minutes."

"Here." Noah handed her cash from his wallet. "Don't use your credit or debit cards. They may be tracking them. And you might want to lose the surgical gown. The less conspicuous you are, the better."

She looked down, the expression of confusion adorable on her face. "Oh yeah. Forgot about that." She shrugged out of the gown and tossed it in the back seat. "Any requests?"

"Ibuprofen and cola. Maybe a bag of pretzels." He wasn't sure his stomach could handle much more.

"Got it."

He watched her walk into the store. Somehow with everything they'd just been through, she moved with confidence, her shiny curls blowing in the breeze. Were they as soft as they looked?

Not that he should be thinking such things, but at least she wasn't engaged. Still, he had nothing to offer any woman but a soiled name and a reputation for failing to protect.

He leaned his head back against the headrest and paid for it with another round of dizziness and pain shooting up his shoulder.

He was in over his head here.

Lord, I haven't thanked you yet for helping me find her. Thank you. Now help me keep her safe. After all the loss my family has caused her, I don't want to hurt her any more.

He released a slow breath, letting calm assurance settle his mind.

Talia came out of the store with two bags and a gallon of water. Noah pushed the button to open the trunk and got out. "Let me help you with that."

"I've got it."

"I know you've got it. I'm trying to be a gentleman here."

"Oh." She handed him the water. It almost slipped out of his hand, but he caught it just in time.

Soon they were back on the road, climbing up out of the foothills to the taller peaks of the Sawtooth Range.

Noah watched the rain, his eyelids slipping closed after a few minutes.

"Is that important to you?" Talia's question broke the silence and woke him.

"Is what important?"

"Being a gentleman."

She was still thinking about that? "I guess it was something my family always drilled into me. You open a door for a lady, help her with heavy loads, give her your seat on a bus, that kind of thing."

"I was fine carrying those groceries on my own."

"By offering to help, I wasn't implying you weren't. It's simply a way to show you respect."

"Is that important to guys?"

"Uh, I can't speak for all of us, but in general, yeah, a guy likes to help a woman out to let her know she can depend on him. Show her honor."

She chewed on her lip as she concentrated on the road, maybe the conversation too. Eventually she spoke up again. "So, it's kind of like when the stallion does something to get the mare's attention?"

"Huh?"

"We don't see it as much in domesticated horses, but in the wild, the mustangs are in harems. It's the stallion's job to protect the mares. He fights off any other males and will often lower his head and neck, and the ears will flatten in a threatening position if another stallion approaches. Is it like that?"

"I'm not fighting off another guy to impress you, Talia. I'm just trying to be nice."

She sighed. "Guess I'll never get it." She shook her head, but then turned to him. "But thank you."

Good thing she turned back to the road. He held in the snicker that almost escaped. She probably wouldn't appreciate him laughing at her, but she was just too cute as she tried to make sense of the intricacies of human social interaction.

It still didn't make sense why Noah, wounded, would feel the need to help her carry a few groceries. She didn't need the help.

And why prove himself a "gentleman"? She knew he was strong and capable. If it hadn't been for him, she would be dead.

She really didn't understand it all. Maybe she didn't deserve to be part of a family. She didn't connect with people they way others seemed to. She couldn't give Danny the intimacy he wanted.

The initial flattery of him overlooking her awkwardness and asking her out eventually wore off. And yet, she tried so hard to make it work with him, to do her hair the way he suggested, wear clothes he picked out for her, even if they were flashier than she liked and uncomfortable.

She hoped it would make her feel normal. To have a boyfriend, plan a family of their own. But deep down, she knew she couldn't make him happy. Other women would talk about romance and fluttery feelings, but she had none of those sensations when it came to Danny or any other guy. It was her fault it didn't work out.

It was probably her fault that Sally was taken too. And now she dragged Noah into this, and he was shot.

She checked the rearview mirrors. At least it looked like they lost their bad guys. Noah needed a place to rest. She needed a place to think.

"How much longer 'til we reach the cabin?" Noah asked.

"Another hour. You should rest."

"I'll rest when we get there. The curvy roads make it hard to zonk out. Do you have anything you want to listen to? Radio?"

"Don't get many radio signals here, and the animal science podcasts I usually listen to would probably put you to sleep. Even Danny can't stand to listen to them, and he's a vet."

"So no on the podcast. Okay. I think the anesthetic is wearing off. Tell me about you. Distract me from this hole in my arm."

Talk about herself? It was hard enough to keep the car on the winding road. Now he wanted story time?

But the man was in pain. If talking helped… "What do you want to know?"

"Did you grow up in the Owyhees?"

"No. We didn't buy the ranch until I was in junior high."

"Where did you live before that? Where'd you grow up?"

"Everywhere. I don't remember much before kindergarten. But I distinctly remember the smell of tuna fish from Jimmy Roberts's lunch inside the cubby next to mine at Dakota Elementary School. That was the first kindergarten class in Seattle, but we soon moved to Tacoma, and I finished the year there. In first grade we stayed in Tacoma but moved school districts. Then we started moving to smaller towns, always heading east. Eventually we came to Idaho. By the time we found Jordan Creek Valley, I had been in twelve different schools."

"Must've been hard."

She shrugged. "Even when I was in a school, the teachers never knew what to do with me. I was above my grade in reading and math skills but couldn't relate to kids my own age. So, they would move me into upper-grade classes for schoolwork, and I had an even harder time with the older students socially. I never really fit in anywhere."

And some things never changed.

"You had to have some friends."

"Just Sally and Sunny. I remember the ranches we would volunteer at on the weekends. That's where I made friends."

"Other horse-lovers?"

"Uh, no, the horses."

"No wonder you're a vet." He said it with a warm smile. The kind that made his eyes crinkle and did funny things to her concentration.

"What can I say? Horses make more sense than people."

He paused. When he spoke again, his voice was low. Soft. "People are complicated."

She glanced at him. Maybe it wasn't just her.

Sometimes it was exhausting trying to figure her fellow human beings out, sort out their true motives from the things they said and did.

But it was kind of comforting to know she wasn't the only one.

FIVE

Talia turned the car on to a dirt road, and they continued to climb. She swerved to avoid the washed-out areas and the worst of the potholes, but the winding back and forth wasn't much better. Noah held his stomach, hoping the pretzels and medicine would stay put. Finally, she stopped the car and announced, "We're here."

Thank the Lord.

Noah opened his door and stood slowly. The dizziness was hardly noticeable. He looked the place over as he moved to the trunk for the groceries. If the road to get here was any indication, it was remote alright. A little log cabin with an attached garage set on a steep incline, tucked among evergreens.

He doubted anyone could find them here.

His arm was screaming at him by the time Talia found the key and he was able to drop the groceries on the small dining room table next to a seventies-style kitchen.

Talia plopped the water jug next to the bags and pointed toward the living room. "You need to go rest. You can lay down in the bedroom or take the couch."

"Are you always so bossy?"

She thought about it for a little bit and then nodded.

"Only when I'm right and I know what needs to be done. Go." She pushed him toward the couch that was calling his name.

No need to resist. His injured body hit its limit. She was protected...for the moment. With that settled, he collapsed on the plush leather sofa under the deer mount and should've fallen asleep to the sounds of Talia putting food away.

The ibuprofen he took in the car helped take the edge off the pain, but questions assaulted his mind long after he closed his eyes.

Who was after Sally and Talia?

How had they found them?

And then snapshots of little Anna Coleson, a week after her fourth birthday, running with Carol from city to city to small town, changing their identity to Talia and Sally Knowles, played in his head. She had such a lonely childhood that she couldn't name a single friend from those days but an old stuffed animal. Of course, the woman could probably name every horse she'd encountered in the twenty-five years since he last saw her.

Kind of sad. But also, amazing. She was different than any other woman he knew. Different in a refreshing and fascinating way.

He thought of Sally. How in the world were they going to find her? If he wasn't bound by his promise to the stubborn woman, he would take Talia to her uncle back in San Jose. Surely Gregory would have plenty of resources to help them find Sally.

But she had been adamant. It was more than a stubborn conviction in Sally's eyes as she pleaded with him to keep the uncle under wraps for now. He couldn't shake it, the desperation in her grip.

He sighed. Because he also remembered sitting in Gregory's plush office, promising Gregory that he could find his niece. Given who Noah's father was, Gregory was reluctant to believe Noah. But Noah did it. And here she was.

Yet Noah saw what Sally meant. Talia was strong, but she needed to find Sally first before he opened up this whole new world to her. Gregory could wait. Sally couldn't. He could wait for a little while, but ultimately, he would do what was best for the woman under his protection. He couldn't fail her like he failed Kelley in Afghanistan. The official report cleared him of any charges, but the translator still died during the skirmish when he was the one tasked to guard her.

So, going to Gregory Coleson was out of the question for the moment. But then, what else could they do to find Sally's kidnappers?

While pondering, he must've fallen asleep, because he woke out of a deep sleep and sat straight up. Vestiges of his nightmare still hanging on, the cruel taunts of classmates colliding with Kelley's screams. The playground at his elementary school swirling with the desert backdrop and the metallic smell of blood stung his nostrils.

You'll follow in his steps! And make a big mess...
Boom!

He scraped his hands down his face. You'd think he'd outgrown the pain. But something of the rhyme always felt true, no matter how many times his mother urged him to ignore it. Like those pictures of animals after an oil spill, he could never quite shake off the black sludge of a dishonored name. He took a few minutes to clear the shouting memories in his head. Once his breathing was back to normal and his pulse had slowed, he stood and stretched. The light outside dimmed as dusk descended on the mountain cabin. He must've slept a few hours.

Now, where was Talia? He sniffed the air. Garlic and oregano drifted from the kitchen. He followed his nose and found her covered in a big plaid apron, pulling a pizza out of the oven.

"Is that homemade?"

She placed the pizza on the table. "Yup. One of the few things I can make. Hungry?"

"Yes!"

He set out a couple plates while she filled glasses with iced tea. He bit into his slice and groaned. "Wow. Now, this is good."

She blushed at his compliment.

"Where'd you learn how to make this? I don't remember your mom cooking much Italian food. And Carol always said it was for good reason she was hired as a nanny rather than the chef for your family."

The rosy blush on her cheeks vanished. Talia's smile fell. What did he say?

She swallowed her bite and took a sip of tea. But the blanched look on her face worried him.

"Talia? What's wrong?"

"She was my nanny?" The last word was a whisper as her throat caught.

Oh no. Not good. He scrambled back over conversations. She didn't know Sally was the nanny? Wasn't the whole aunt title just a show of love and respect?

"Noah, tell me the truth. Are you saying Sally isn't my aunt?"

How much did he reveal? "She's your family. That's all that matters. And I'll help you find her."

"But is she my father's sister? My last living relative?"

She wouldn't let it drop. The woman before him was as tenacious as the preschooler he remembered. He set his pizza down and laid his hand on hers. It was cold and clammy. Her face was even whiter. "Look, Sally raised you. She loves you. That's the kind of family you have."

"That may be." She clenched a fist around her napkin. "But I would still like to know the truth. Who is Sally in relation to me?"

For all the truth he couldn't tell her now, he probably owed her this. He shifted in his seat but maintained eye contact. "She's not your *real* aunt. She was your nanny. But all you need to know is that she lived her whole life keeping you safe, loving you. That's what family does. And we're going to find her."

She stared back at him for a few seconds. Then with a slow nod, she said in a quiet voice, "Thank you for telling me the truth." She stood and walked out the French doors to the log railing deck.

Noah's pizza settled hard in his stomach. He wasn't sure if that was the right thing to do, but he could see now why Sally wanted to be the one to tell Talia about Gregory and give her time to slowly let her digest the truth about the family that she couldn't remember. Talia didn't take change very well.

Shouldn't be surprised. Talia said it herself. She didn't improvise.

And here he just shook her whole world, her sense of family and identity with this one revelation.

What would she do when she found out the rest?

Talia paced back and forth on the deck. When they'd talked about Sally earlier, it didn't click. But one simple word made all the difference.

Her nanny.

Nanny Carol.

Another piece fit into the empty places of her past. But in doing so, it shifted the whole structure, and she'd yet to find a way to make it stop shaking.

With each step, the truth sank in a little deeper.

Not her aunt. Her nanny.

Waves of emotion ebbed and flowed. Emotions she couldn't name. Emotions she couldn't control or understand.

She continued pacing.

Nanny Carol.

Images of Sally… Carol…whoever she was…spun through her head. The woman who tended her through sickness, who found stables and horses no matter where they lived. The woman who championed for her in each school she attended, making sure she was challenged and learning. The woman who patiently explained the strange ways humans interacted and helped her navigate this overwhelming world.

Maybe Noah was right, and that's the kind of family that really mattered.

But if Sally wasn't her aunt, then she didn't have even one blood relative on this earth. Not one. The truth left such a gaping hole inside, she could hardly breathe.

So strange that she should feel this way. Made no logical sense. She was the same person she was last week, yesterday, or even earlier this morning. But now she realized how alone she was in this world, and the one person she trusted the most had lied to her.

A sense of loss.

That's what Sally would say it was. Like when Custer died. To some he might've been just a horse. To her he was the first friend she lost. Something about discovering Sally was no blood relation produced the same sensation.

And it threatened to overwhelm her.

Talia needed something else to concentrate on.

Aunt or nanny, she was still the only person who really knew Talia. And although she probably did it for her own good, it was time for Sally to reveal the truth about her real family. All the questions she put off needed answers. Sally had them.

Talia marched back into the cabin and found Noah standing at the kitchen sink. "We need to find Sally."

"Yeah. I've been racking my brain trying to think of how we could track her down."

"And?"

"I might know somebody who can help. One of my marine buddies is a federal agent—"

"Call him."

Using the number off his cell phone, he called on the avocado-green landline hanging on the wall in the kitchen.

"Hey, Justin. It's Noah Landers. I was wondering if you could help me out." He gave a quick rundown of what happened that morning. It was accurate. Precise. Something she could appreciate.

As soon as he hung up, Talia popped up. "Will he help? Can he?"

"He thinks he can access some satellite footage from this morning, see if there was any coverage over Sally's ranch, but he didn't hold out much hope. It's such a remote area, and unless there's something worth monitoring…they won't have anything. But he's going to look into… Talia? Did I lose you?"

Coverage over the ranch. Of course!

She grabbed the phone off the wall and started dialing.

"Who are you calling?" Noah asked.

"Someone who might have coverage over the ranch."

"They have access to satellite images?"

"No."

A monotone voice answered the phone. "Western Idaho Community College. How may I direct your call?"

"Dr. Paul Stanton. And it's urgent. Tell him this is Dr. Talia Knowles."

He picked up. "Dr. Knowles. What can I do—"

"Tell me you still have drone footage over the Owyhees while you track the mustangs. Specifically over Jordan Valley?"

"I'll need to check with my students. But we do have some ranches we're monitoring in that area. What are we looking for? Missing livestock?"

"No. My…aunt was taken from her ranch this morning. Two black SUVs. According to my watch it was 8:36 a.m. on Red Canyon Road. The Mustang Sally Ranch. If you have any footage over that road from this morning, then you could help us find her. Even if we can narrow down which way they went at the crossroads of Owyhee County Road 3 and Falcon Road, it would be a huge help."

"I'll get right on it, but it will take me a while. I have to contact my students and see if any of them were monitoring that area at that specific time. How can I reach you?"

She gave him the cabin number written on the phone and hung up. Resumed her pacing. She should've thought of it sooner. They'd lost valuable time. And now all they could do was wait.

Another wave of…something hit. Aunt Sally. Nanny Carol. How did she not see that before? Her slight accent that came out on a few occasions alone should've clued her in. And why had Sally lied all this time?

Truth was important. Facts didn't change. They weren't relative or subjective. That's why they made sense. What could she do with this idea that Sally, who knew how important truth was, lied to her?

What else did she lie about?

She looked over at the handsome cowboy leaning against the counter, watching her.

At least Noah told her the truth.

The woman was a bundle of barely harnessed energy as she continued rocking on her feet, staring at him…or maybe it was more like through him. He needed to tell her the rest of what was going on, but she was barely holding it together.

"You doing okay, Talia?"

She startled. "Yes, I'm fine."

They needed a task. Something to ground her. "How about we put together that list the sheriff asked for?"

"List?"

"Of people who might be after you."

"I don't know anyone that would kidnap Sally and shoot out my house. I'm oblivious to a lot, but no one hates me that much."

"Maybe you stumbled onto something and don't even know it."

"Something worth kidnapping Sally?"

"You never know." He pulled out a chair at the dining room table for her, but she shook her head.

"I think better on my feet."

"Okay, let's start with work. How's that going?"

"Fine. It's just me, a couple vet techs and a receptionist who covers the front desk and keeps us organized."

"Any patients' owners that might be angry with you?"

She balked. "No! I take excellent care of my patients."

"How about your research? What are you studying with the mustangs?"

"I help with the horse land management for the state. There's a number of wild horses but only enough public land in the management acreage to sustain a percentage of that. I help at one of the holding facilities, checking over the animals, helping decide which are healthy for adoption, making sure the mustangs are being handled appropriately. We also microchip them before we release them back into the wild. I track their movements."

She looked over his shoulder at something and started pacing again, tapping her fingers on her leg. The gears were turning.

"Talia?"

No response.

"Talia!"

"What?" she answered, but still no eye contact.

"Your research?"

"I just never thought it would come to anything."

"What are you talking about?"

"I did receive some anonymous threats. I thought they were just scare tactics or jokes."

"When?"

"The last one was seventeen days ago."

"First of all, I can't believe you remember the exact

number of days, but more importantly, what kind of threat?"

"I received letters at my practice, threatening me to back off the governor's office. I've been trying to put pressure on them to add more funding to the mustang holding facilities and to better regulate them. And I turned in one manager who was abusing the horses. He might not be too happy with me either."

"Do you think that's what Sally meant by the 'key equals mustangs'?"

"I don't see how. I didn't tell her."

"Why not?"

"It didn't occur to me that the threats were serious. I thought they were a hoax. Who doesn't sign a letter?"

"Okay, we still need to look into these leads. Who was the manager you turned in?"

"Dwight Quincy."

"Good. Now we have a name to give Sheriff Daniels. What about the ranch? Anybody that Sally has a disagreement with?"

"No one I can think of. We keep to ourselves and help out our—" she gasped. "Neighbors!"

"What's wrong?"

"I forgot to call the Polecheski brothers and ask them to watch over Peaches. We'll need someone to do chores too, take care of the others!"

"It's okay—"

"No, it's not okay! How could I forget them?" She rushed to the phone and called the neighboring ranch.

"Alice? It's Talia… You saw Peaches there? Is she okay?" She arranged for the neighbors to cover the chores and watch over Sally's ranch. She also let them know Noah was there too, staying to protect her.

After she hung up, she resumed her laps between the small dining area and the living room. Faster than before.

He almost had her calmed down with the list, but now she was more distraught than ever, and there was still so much more to tell her. "Talia, anyone else we can add to this list?"

"I don't think so," she said without looking at him. Her voice barely registering.

"Why don't you come and try to eat a little more. We need to keep up your strength. And your pizza tastes incredible, even cold." He gave her his most charming smile, the one that showed off that dimple his mother said could entice the spots off a pinto.

But it was wasted effort. She came and sat down without a glance at him. She nibbled on her slice for a bit before she stood and resumed her back-and-forth march.

Dusk turned to dark outside the French doors, the outline of the trees black against the indigo-blue sky. There wouldn't be much they could do now but rest and come up with a plan of action for tomorrow.

He watched Talia's ponytail bob with each step, her slender fingers tapping her thigh as she walked.

"Talia, why don't we call the sheriff, give him this information and settle in for the night?"

"How am I supposed to settle in when I don't know where Sally is? I don't know how my animals are."

"Do you trust the Polecheski brothers?"

She stopped and made eye contact. Improvement.

"Yes. They take good care of the animals, maintain clean barns, use quality feed."

"So your animals are in good hands. That much we can know. And the sooner we get this information to the sheriff, the more leads they can run down in finding Sally."

"True."

She reached for the phone and called the county office, giving Sheriff Daniels the name of the shady manager and telling him about the threats she received. When she was done, she walked out to the deck and leaned over the railing, staring into the forest surrounding them. Better than the nervous pacing.

He was usually great with people, but something about her posture told him she didn't need him to fill up the silence with empty platitudes. He turned off the dining room lights. It would be better to see the stars that way. Then, he simply went and stood next to her.

Water somewhere nearby gurgled and rushed down the mountain. Must be a creek or river on the property. A cold breeze rustled the towering pine trees all around them.

"We have to find her, Noah," she said. Her voice small, tight. It lingered in the air.

An intense desire welled up inside him. A desire to clear away all the pain that lurked behind her words. "I know. And we're going to do everything we can to make that happen."

"But will it be enough?" She stared at him, her blue eyes begging him for assurance.

All he had was the truth. "I don't know."

With a slow nod and a slight lift to her lips, she sighed. "Thank you for telling me the truth. I may want certainty, but truth is more important."

"Guess that's why they call it faith, huh." He turned and leaned his elbows on the railing, looked up at the sky and found the Big Dipper.

She looked up too. "Faith. Not something I've ever been comfortable with. I prefer facts."

"We need both."

"Maybe. But I'd rather stick to truth. And the truth is, for many years Sally lied to me. I'm not sure what to do with that."

"But you have faith that she's worth looking for."

"It's not faith. It's the fact that she's the one with answers. I want to know the truth about my family. I might've been content to be ignorant in the past, thinking she was protecting me. Now I need to know. So, thank you for helping me, and thank you for telling me the truth."

She kissed him on the cheek. He caught a whiff of some floral scent, maybe her shampoo. The sweet gesture took him by surprise, but despair rooted his boots to the deck when she walked away. He watched her through the glass as she cleared the table.

He hung his head and kicked the pine cone at his foot. He should soak in her kind words and sweet kiss now.

She would hate him before this was all over.

SIX

Talia carried the glasses from the dark dining room to the brightly lit kitchen sink and set them on the counter. She stared at her reflection in the window. What had gotten into her? She could still smell the slightly musky all-masculine scent of Noah, feel the roughness of his stubble on her lips.

She'd kissed Noah.

Voluntarily.

Yeah, it was just the cheek, but where had that come from?

She ran water in the dishpan and added a squirt of soap.

Lack of physical touch was one of the things Danny complained about. It meant more to him or something. She didn't mind the hand-holding or kissing with him, but she was fine without it too.

He wasn't happy that he always had to initiate it. Nor could he understand that it wasn't on her radar when she was with him.

A mound of bubbles in the sink grew until she turned the water off. She had tried keeping a mental checklist: ask about his day—not just his patients, make an effort to notice any physical changes, compliment his work, etc. But initiating some form of physical contact always fell through the cracks.

And here, out of the blue, she couldn't help but wonder what it would be like to kiss Noah. Like, really kiss him.

She never once felt that way about her ex-fiancé.

It only confirmed that she was right to call off the wedding.

A passion for veterinary medicine and someone who seemed attracted to her was not enough to build a marriage.

Maybe it had been more about making her feel normal. Danny was a great vet. They had intelligent conversations. But he wanted more. A more she couldn't offer.

She wasn't marriage material. She wasn't the kind of woman that men wanted. She couldn't read them. Give them that emotional connection. She needed to stick to what she knew. Animals. Horses. Forget men or any silly notion of marriage.

Or a family of her own.

She shook herself as she cleared the last plate from the table and brought it to the sink.

Noah rushed in. "Kill the lights!"

"What?"

He ran to the living room lamp and turned it off, then rushed to her, grabbing her and swinging her around so he could reach the switch behind her. He held her close in the dark.

"What's going on?" And why did being in his arms affect her breathing so?

"I heard a helicopter outside. It could be nothing, but

as serious as these guys are, they could be looking for us by air now."

"How would they know we're here?"

"I don't know. Maybe they followed us to the highway and guessed we're hiding in the mountains. I saw a search beam. Whoever is in the bird is looking for something."

He continued to hold her in the dark. Her hand rested on his arm, the wiry muscles taut beneath her fingers. He was strong, his breath steady, while her heart beat as fast as a hummingbird's.

Sure enough, the rhythmic *whomp-whomp* of a helicopter's blades grew louder. Her breath caught in her throat, and she squeezed Noah's arm. He pulled her a little closer, wrapping her in his strong hold, a hint of masculine evergreen scent tickling her nose.

Outside the kitchen window, a beam of light sliced the night. It swept over the trees and then the driveway. The chopper grew louder. Was it just her imagination or did it seem to linger right above them?

"What do we do?" she whispered.

"Try to stay calm and wait."

"But what if it's them?"

"If it is, we run. But if we make a move now, they'll see us. Thankfully the car is hidden in the garage, and I think we turned the lights off in time. So, we wait."

Talia closed her eyes and prayed.

Eventually the helicopter moved on, and the noise faded away.

Noah loosened his hold, but she was reluctant to leave him. "Are we safe?"

"I think so. They would've landed to investigate if they thought we were here. But that was a close call.

Our headlights will give us away if we try to leave now, and no way can we navigate that mountain road without them. So we'll have to leave first thing in the morning."

"Okay." As her pulse returned to normal, she started shaking.

"Hey, Talia, we're fine now." Noah led her to the chair.

She sat, but the shivering grew worse. "I know that logically, but my body seems to be going through a bit of shock. It's the adrenaline response."

"What can I do?"

"I'll be fine. I just need to rest. I can't handle anything else right now."

He smoothed a curl from her forehead, his touch soothing and gentle. "Go ahead and lie down. I'll stay up and keep watch for a while. We should be safe until morning."

Looking in his eyes, she believed him in one sense. She *would* be physically safe with Noah Landers. He was smart, strong, capable. But she was coming to depend on him way too much. This new yearning to be with him was throwing her whole world off balance. Her peace of mind—some might say her heart—was definitely at risk.

She stood and fled from his presence, calling behind her, "I need some sleep. See you in the morning."

Talia jolted out of bed. The phone was ringing! She rushed to the kitchen landline, blinking to clear the sleep and blurry vision from her eyes. The sun wasn't up, but the inky-black sky outside the window was fading to a dull gray above the treetops. A glance at her watch as she answered the phone told her it was 5:57 a.m.

"Hello?"

"Talia, it's Paul. Sorry it's so early, but I knew you'd be anxious to get the information on your aunt's ranch. Some students and I scanned all the drone footage we could find. We didn't have any directly over your aunt's ranch, but we tracked the SUVs to the crossroads you mentioned. They turned east. We're not sure because it was farther away, but we think they headed north later. They were on Happy Valley Road which would take them right into the city of Nampa."

"Happy Valley Road. Okay."

"Hope that helps. I wish we could've gotten back to you last night, but it took a while to find my student who has the footage over that area."

"It helps a great deal. Could you do me another favor and send that footage to Sheriff Daniels of Owyhee County?"

"Of course. I hope your aunt is okay."

"Thank you."

Finally. A lead.

She hung up the phone and started a pot of coffee.

Of course, that lead was almost twenty-four hours old. Maybe the information was useless.

No. Information was never useless. Tracking the kidnappers to Nampa put them on their trail. Facts. Truths.

So much better than speculation.

"Who called?"

She jumped and spun around, spilling coffee grounds on the wood-planked floor.

It must've been the surprise that caused her heart rate to accelerate. It had nothing to do with seeing Noah standing there barefoot in his jeans and a rather thin T-shirt molded to his muscular chest and arms. Nothing to do with the handsome jaw lined with a dark scruff, or big brown eyes that probed her as she dropped to the floor with a rag and tried brushing the grounds into a pile.

"Uh…it was Dr. Stanton from the college. He has some footage from the time Sally was taken. It shows the SUVs turning east at the crossroads and then later north on Happy Valley Road. They wouldn't have coverage of Nampa, but that's the direction they were heading."

He squatted down beside her, took the rag from her hand, and carried it to the sink, where he rinsed it out. "It's a good place to start. And it was quiet last night after the helicopter left, but we shouldn't stay here any longer. Let me get dressed, and we can head to Nampa."

He started to turn away as she blurted, "Did you sleep okay?" She cleared her throat. "I mean, did your wound cause any pain last night?"

A half smile slid up his cheek. "You worried about me, Doc?"

She stood, heat crawling up her neck. "No, I just… wanted to make sure you're rested and ready for this. Your arm. How is it?"

He looked down at his bandage, drawing her attention to the sculpted shoulder. She swallowed hard.

He shrugged. "I'll be alright."

His smile and groggy morning voice sure did funny things to her stomach. What in the world had gotten into her?

Back to important matters. He was a patient. She pointed to the bar stool at the counter. "I need to change your bandage and check your wound. Then we can leave."

"You're the doc." He sat as directed.

She took a step closer and only let her eyes focus

on the white bandage. His scent, masculine and clean, teased her. She pulled the tape free from his arm and removed the gauze.

He flinched.

"Sorry!"

She looked up and met his eyes. They were such a warm brown. And those lashes. He did the puppy-eyed thing so well.

"How's it look?" he asked, his voice still hoarse and low.

"Good."

"Just good?"

"Yup." She slapped a new bandage over the wound and rushed from the kitchen before her cheeks could burn any brighter.

So this was what physical attraction felt like.

Oh, Lord. Help me now.

Noah chuckled as she left the room. He shouldn't flirt with her, but she was kind of fun to tease. It reminded him of the good old days running around the Coleson place with Xander, spying on his older sisters and sometimes trying to ditch tagalong Anna by riling her up until she threw a fit and left them.

Although now, he didn't want her to leave.

Not like he'd have a chance with her or any other woman, for that matter. Not after she found out the truth about whose son he was. Or what chaos seemed to follow in his wake. No matter how much she blushed at his teasing.

He grunted as he reached for his boot with his bad arm. It was better than yesterday, but he was still ready for some ibuprofen. Then again, maybe he shouldn't try to take the edge off the pain. Maybe it would kick some sense into him.

Eventually he needed to tell Talia the rest of her story, about her uncle, about his dad. And despite what Sally thought, Talia deserved to know she still had family. But after the helicopter scare last night, he could tell she had hit her limit. Hopefully, after a good night's sleep, she was recovered and ready for the whole story. The ride down would be a good opportunity, but he should offer to drive.

He pulled on his socks and boots and folded the blanket he'd used on the couch, straightened up the room and chugged down a mug of coffee before Talia emerged.

She brought him a cotton plaid shirt and thick flannel jacket. "Take these. I know this couple, and they would want you to have them. They will help you stay warm since we left your bloody ones at the animal hospital."

"I'll be okay. Maybe we can stop at—"

"Take them. Don't be some dumb cowboy that has to prove how tough he is." She threw them at him and walked away, shaking her head.

Gotta love a woman with spark.

Without much more talking, except to argue over who was driving, they locked up the cabin once more and pulled back onto the mountain road just as the sky was turning gold in the east.

"So, what's the plan, Doc?" Noah asked from the driver's seat.

Talia glared at him. Probably still upset about him winning the coin toss and getting behind the wheel. "Head to Nampa. As soon as we get reception, I'll pull up a map, and we can see what's along Happy Valley Road. Of course, they may have just headed toward the interstate, and who knows where they would go from there."

"They're after you, though. I don't think they'd go too far."

Her glare disappeared. "You think they're after me?"

"Yes. They asked about a girl. You're the only one in Sally's life. Not that you're a girl, but you know what I mean. Then they shot up *your* house and found us at the animal hospital. It's all tied to you."

"Then they probably took Sally for leverage." She sighed, and her brows knotted up yet again.

"That would be my guess. But that's good. They'll keep her alive as long as they're looking for you and think they can use her to lure you out."

She glanced over, her forehead relaxing a little. "You really believe that, or are you trying to make me feel better?"

"I believe it. They could've killed Sally on her front porch if they wanted. They didn't."

"You have valid logic." Her shoulders relaxed a tad. "But I still feel…"

"Scared?"

"Yes. I am."

"That's normal, Talia. You're in danger."

"But I hate feeling this way. It's all out of my control. And I don't even know why they're after me. We don't know who they are or where they took Sally."

"I know." And he'd like to promise her he wouldn't let any harm come to her. But for all his talk of faith, he still worried. Worried that he would follow in his dad's footsteps and fail her. Worried that he would never know what part his father played in her family's deaths.

"Tell me about my family, Noah. I don't remember

them. I need details. I know what kind of people they were. Sally did her best to keep the memory of what they were like alive, but she wouldn't give me details. I don't—" She huffed. "I don't even remember names. Except for Xander, and that's because you told me. I don't need the fluffy stuff right now. I want facts."

The woman continued to surprise him. And if anyone understood the need for answers, it was him. "Okay. Your parents were Doug and Colleen Coleson. Your father was on the cutting edge of navigational technology and started the Coleson Company in Silicon Valley. He was really smart. I always thought your dad was a cool father. Xander, being the only boy, would go on these hiking trips with your dad, and I got to go along. We had a blast."

"And my mom?"

"Your mom, Colleen, stayed at home with you and your brother and sisters and was very involved in the community. She would have us help at different events and charity fundraisers. I hated dressing up for them, but we always got to eat leftover desserts. She threw great parties too. She was organized, always had her planner. And she laughed a lot."

He told her about her two older sisters Alena and Ava, and Xander. What they looked like, the games they would play.

Her smile softened the hard lines in her forehead. It took all his self-control to not touch the wisp of a curl that hugged her cheek.

Eyes on the road.

He continued to answer her questions and share the details she wanted while winding their way down the mountain, the white water of the river cutting into the gorge below on one side of the road and the mountain face on the other.

With a glimmer of unshed tears in her eyes, she glanced at him for a moment. "Thank you. Those were exactly the kind of details I needed to hear. It's probably weird to ask about their height and eye color, but it makes them seem more like real people. Not just make-believe characters in some story."

Making her smile was a new kind of joy. But he needed to tell her the rest, and it would probably wipe that smile right off her beautiful face, but she deserved to know.

He took a deep breath. "There's more you should know, Talia. My father—well, he died before anything could ever be proven, but some think he was responsible for killing your family. I was looking for you and Sally because you two were probably the last ones to see him alive. And because—"

Talia screamed. "Watch out!"

SEVEN

A black SUV swerved into their path and sped straight toward them. Sheer terror ripped through Talia's heart, her body paralyzed. Guardrails sped past in her peripheral vision. She couldn't look away from the hulking SUV in their path.

She screamed again, and watched Noah narrow his eyes and adjust his grip. At the last second, he jerked the steering wheel, then straightened it again, and they slipped past the vehicle. Talia whipped around to see the SUV squeal on its tires as it spun in a one-eighty behind them and continued the chase.

She pounded on center console. "Go! Go! Go!"

Noah said nothing, but they picked up speed as they rounded a curve. Another look back and the SUV was on their tail. She braced herself for impact, but the crossover engine revved. Noah kept them in their lane as they flew past more cars.

"What do we do?" And how was the man not freaking out?

"Hang on." His jaw clenched tight.

"What?"

"Hang on to something."

Talia barely had a chance to grab the door handle when her seat belt locked, pinning her to the back of the seat. She squeezed her eyes shut and felt the car brake, spin around and come to a stop. When she opened her eyes again, her chest was heaving, and her hands were squeezing the handle so tight, her fingers were white. She looked around. Somehow Noah had swung the car into a scenic overlook at the side of the road, thankfully empty of tourists and photographers.

The SUV flew past them, brakes screeching, and smoke trailing from its tires as it tried to stop and navigate the sharp curve in the road ahead. Instead the vehicle fishtailed, toppled, and rolled down the side of the mountain into the river below.

When Talia caught her breath again, she turned to Noah. "Where did you learn to drive like that?"

"I learned how to drive in the mountains near our ranch. Teaches you a thing or two. Are you okay?" His brow wrinkled as he looked her over.

She loosened her seat belt, could feel bruising and a burn where the strap had been, but one look at the black tire marks in the road in front of them veering off the road and she nodded. "I'm fine."

"Good, because we better go before those guys call for backup."

Cars coming from the opposite direction had already pulled over, some of the drivers getting out, on their phones, most likely calling for help. Noah maneuvered around them, and they continued toward Nampa.

Her heart rate returned to normal, but her thoughts were still caught in a tailspin.

Wait. He said his father might be responsible for the death of her family? And not just death. He said, *kill-*

ing of your family. But Sally told her they died in a car accident.

Before she could sort it all out, Noah's phone rang, interrupting her thoughts. They must be back in cell phone reception range.

He held the phone to his ear. "Justin? Yeah, we left the cabin a while ago and ran into some trouble… We're fine now, although looks like they're back on our trail. We found some drone footage and know that after taking Sally, the SUVs headed into Nampa on Happy Valley Road. Any chance you have satellite footage over the city?"

She tried to be patient as Noah said little more than "Yup. Uh-huh. Okay." But her lips pinched tighter the longer it took.

Noah continued. "You're sure?… Yes. That's got to be them… Don't worry, I'll be careful… Thanks, man. I owe ya." He ended the call and turned toward her. "Once I gave him those road names, Justin tracked them to the Nampa Airport. The SUVs pulled into one of the private hangars, and he gave me the number of the building. Looks like only one of them left earlier this morning. That must be our friends in the river. The other SUV hasn't left."

"Then we should go to the airport."

"He's going to contact the local law enforcement, but we're close. I thought we could scope out the hangar, see if we can find Sally."

"Justin was okay with that?"

"Didn't really give him a choice. He'd do the same if he was in my shoes. Besides, most likely there will be too many men for us to fight off. I just want to do some recon."

"But what if we find Sally? We can't just leave her there."

"I know, but it might be better if we wait for backup. We may find her and then have to let the police or FBI, whoever Justin can get on the case, take over."

Was he serious? "No, if we find her, we need to find a way to free her."

"Talia, we can't bust in there alone. We have one gun between us, and I'm injured. It would cause more danger for her and you. These guys are serious. I just want to see what we're up against."

"I left her once to fight these guys off by herself. I'm not going to leave her again."

"Yeah, but remember, they're probably using her to get to you. You run in there and get caught and they'll have no more reason to keep her alive. In fact, maybe you should stay put somewhere while I check things out, and I promise, if I can get her out safely, I will."

"No way! You're not going anywhere without me. If Sally's there, I'm going with you."

He looked in the rearview mirror and muttered something about being stubborn as a mule.

"Mutter all you want. Mules happened to be very intelligent and sure-footed creatures."

"Fine. But we can't just waltz up there. Justin said there's a museum next to the airport. We'll park there. If it's clear, we'll stroll across the street to the hangars. And we'll only do recon. Deal?"

He was probably right in being out-manned and out-gunned. Reconnaissance was better than nothing. "Deal. But then I need to hear the rest of the story about your father and my family. It doesn't make sense."

"I know. And I think Sally has a lot of the answers we're both looking for. So let's go see if she's here."

He pulled into the parking lot of the Warhawk Air Museum right next to the small Nampa airport. The sun was still low and the shadows long. The valley was waking up, though, plenty of traffic noise surrounding them, but not enough to drown out the fast beating of her heart as Noah grabbed her hand when she got out of the car.

It beat even faster when a deep voice shouted behind them, "You folks shouldn't be here."

Noah spun around and threw an arm around her back as a uniformed man approached. "My girlfriend and I are here to check out the World War II display."

The security officer walked up to them. "The museum doesn't open for another forty-five minutes."

Noah looked at her. "Oh, that's too bad. Hey, babe, don't our friends own one of those hangars over there? What do you say we check it out and come back a little later?"

She nodded. All thoughts fled when he looked at her like that. She was too aware of the way his hand slid from her shoulder to the small of her back. Hopefully the officer bought into Noah's natural charm, because she could not come up with one coherent thought.

The guard looked confused. "Not much to see over there by the hangars, but the museum does have a great display. Come on back at nine."

Noah took her hand again. "We'll be back once it's open." He turned and led her across the street at a leisurely trot.

Talia looked behind her and watched the guard continue his rounds. "Do you think he bought it?"

"I think so. Come on." As soon as they reached the

corner of the first hangar and were out of sight, they broke into a jog and ran the length of the building. There were five rows of hangars, and the one Justin said he tracked the SUVs to was located at the opposite end.

Once they reached it, Noah leaned over to whisper directly in her ear. "Let's approach it from the back, see if there are any windows or doors. Stay behind me and stay quiet."

He let go of her hand, and a chill replaced his warmth. They walked along the metal-sided building. A breeze whipped up the same time a plane engine started down the runway nearby. They found a small window in the back wall of the hangar, but it was too high to reach.

Noah locked his fingers together, making a foothold as if he were going to boost her up onto the back of a horse. "Climb up and see if you can open it."

"No. You'll rip your sutures."

"Come on, we don't have much time. Hop up."

She folded her arms. "I'm not going to undo all the work I did yesterday on your arm."

He blew out a quick breath and rolled his eyes. "You are about the most stubborn woman I know." He kneeled on the ground and gave her a knee to step on.

"Thank you." Like Sally always said, that determination got her through a lot. She wouldn't apologize for it.

She stepped on Noah's thigh, then up onto his shoulders, and reached the window. Blinds covered it, leaving no sight lines. She grabbed the lip of the window and tugged to the side. Nothing. What was it about stupid windows getting in her way? "I can't see anything, and it won't open."

"Try again. Use that stubbornness of yours."

She tried sliding it again. The latch lock on the inside moved a little. Maybe she could maneuver that latch enough to unlock it. She pushed on the window again, sliding it up and down with what little give there was in the frame. Each time the latch slid a little more. After a few more wiggles, the latch clicked into the unlocked position, and she slid the window open.

She peeked between the blinds. An office. A desk and chair sat right below the window, one wall lined with shelves, filled with books. Airplane posters and diagrams lined the other wall, and a door across the room from her was cracked open to the main hangar. Through the sliver, she saw a small white jet. Voices on the other side of the door echoed but were muffled enough that she couldn't understand them. She found the string and opened the blinds to keep the wind from knocking them around and alerting anyone.

Noah whispered beneath her. "What is it? What do you see?"

"It's an office. I can see a jet in the hangar, and I hear voices, but I don't see Sally. I need a closer look."

"It's too dangerous! You go in there and you'll be trapped."

Just as Talia was about to hop down and go toe-to-toe with him, voices sounded from around the corner of the building.

"Someone's coming, Talia. Get down," Noah whispered.

Talia looked behind her. They were in the open. Nothing but a chain-link fence behind them and to the side, which must run the length of the hangars. A wide open field with yellowed grasses beyond the fence offered no cover. There was nowhere to hide.

She pushed off Noah's good shoulder, ducked her

head and torso into the opening, and wrapped one leg around the casement.

"What are you doing?" he hissed.

The voices and heavy footsteps drew closer. Cigarette smoke carried on the wind.

"I'm going in."

"I can't reach that window. How am I supposed to protect you?"

The voices were close enough to hear their words.

"Go!" She shooed Noah away as she drew her other leg in and dropped onto the leather office chair. She quietly closed the window and got one last glimpse of Noah before he sprinted away and around the corner, the only hiding place available.

He wouldn't go far. If he stayed in front of the guys and out of sight, he'd be okay. But now she was stuck.

She slipped around the desk and cracked open the door leading to the main hangar.

Might as well make the most of it and see if she could find Sally.

As soon as Talia disappeared from his sight, Noah felt it in his gut. He'd made the wrong choice thinking he could keep her safe.

Adrenaline zipped through his body as he ran around the building. He needed to get into that hangar and protect Talia. A glimpse around the corner showed three men taking a cigarette break right under the window Talia had disappeared through.

Great. They didn't seem worried as they chatted and smoked. But he'd have to find another way in.

He continued around to the front of the steel building. The big door spanning almost the whole length of the hangar was closed. A smaller door next to it was also locked, but the window in it gave him a peek inside at least. A luxury private jet stood gleaming under bright lights, and next to it was a shiny black SUV. Two more guys sat at a table in one corner, smoking and playing cards. The jet and SUV blocked the rest of the room. No sign of Sally or Talia.

Suddenly, one of the men bolted off his chair, and the others followed. They scattered, one moving right toward Noah. Noah ducked and ran back around the corner of the building. Something startled those men. And Talia was trapped inside.

He needed in there now.

He rushed back and looked around the corner where the three men stood under the window Talia used. A voice on a radio of some sort shouted. The men, now on high alert, put out their cigarettes and ran back around the way they had come.

He eyed the window Talia used. If it weren't for his gunshot wound, he probably could jump and hoist himself up, but the way his upper arm throbbed without moving it, he didn't have the strength.

He did another full turn, searching for anything he could use as a stool. The chain-link fence was too far away to use. No boxes or rocks for a boost. Just a bunch of dry grass bowing down in the wind.

He stopped at the neighboring hangar. A door on the back wall was locked but looked flimsy. He could kick it in. There had to be something inside it that he could use.

But should he break into someone else's hangar?

A feminine scream ripped the silence.

Talia!

Without another thought, Noah dashed back to the

original building. He gauged the distance to the little window he last saw Talia disappear through.

With a quick inhale, he pushed off into a sprint. Leaped. Grabbed the windowsill and pulled himself up. His shoulder screamed, something tore, and his Stetson was knocked off, but he held himself up long enough to fit his head and chest into the opening and swing his leg up.

He dropped into the office and moved to the door that opened into the main hangar area. Shouts of the men echoed off the metal siding and high ceilings. A quick look out the doorway showed no place to hide and no sign of Talia. The huge hangar door started rolling up at the same time the jet engines started rumbling.

Was Talia in the plane?

One more guy, bulky, wearing all black, ran up the steps and into the plane. He might've been the same guy that chased them down at the animal hospital. Before Noah could get a better look at his face, he lifted the stairs and closed the door to the jet.

No! She could be in there!

The plane wheeled out of the hangar and moved toward the runway. Two more men guarded it as it left. As soon as it cleared the hangar they moved toward the vehicle.

Noah's head dropped to his fist, clenched against the door frame. He'd failed. Hadn't gotten inside in time. He fought the urge to punch something.

A flash of movement under the SUV caught his eye when he looked up. Light curly hair and big blue eyes.

Talia.

The pressure in his chest eased. Thank God.

What in the world was she doing under there?

Didn't matter. At least she wasn't on that plane. If she

stayed hidden, they'd be okay. They could wait them out. Eventually they'd go for another smoke break, right?

But instead of leaving, the men opened the doors and started searching for something in the back seat of the car.

Come on. Why didn't they just go?

One of them opened the hatchback. "She's gotta be here. The tracking device says she's right here."

Tracking device?

Talia shook her head slightly, that look of fear as the realization sunk in. They knew she was here. It was just a matter of time.

The other guy tossed a jacket to the side and looked under the seats. "Where else could she be?"

Maybe they were dumb enough to miss her.

"Dude, we gotta go. Kim said cops are on the way."

"Yeah, but you heard the boss. We need to find her before we can go. She's here. Somewhere." The guy turned, looked all around. He looked down at his phone, scratching his head.

And then he figured it out. He rolled his eyes and squatted. Pulled out a gun and pointed it right at Talia's head. "Get out here. Now!"

Outside on the runway, the jet took off and arced high into the sky. No help in sight. No sirens to signal that the cavalry had arrived.

He was Talia's only hope.

If it was just these two, maybe Noah could take them. He looked down. His arm was bleeding again. She was staring at him, her fingers signaling him to run as she made her way out from under the SUV at gunpoint.

But he wasn't going to leave her again.

He stepped out of the office and into the cavernous hangar. "Leave her alone. Take me."

* * *

Talia wanted to scream as she stood up. What was he doing, giving himself up like this?

Noah moved slowly toward them, hands raised in surrender, one not quite as high as the other. Blood stained the upper sleeve of his shirt, dripping on the epoxy floor. He must've ripped his sutures.

Why was he risking himself like this? He should've just followed them and found a way to get word to the police or something.

The last two men in the group, left behind to bring her to their boss, now stood on either side of her and had their guns pointed at Noah.

Noah stepped forward, taking his time. "Look, I don't know what you want with her, but take me instead. I'll do whatever you need."

Jerk Number One swung and pointed his gun on her. "Nice try, but you're not the one the boss wants. We have no use for you."

Jerk Number Two kept his weapon aimed at Noah. His trigger finger twitched.

Talia screamed. "No!" She shoved his arm as the shot went off. A deafening *boom* echoed in the hangar. Noah dropped and rolled. He didn't move.

The two strangers at her side fell to the ground.

What?

Talia rushed forward, kneeling next to Noah's body as an army of black marched in behind her.

EIGHT

No! Talia leaned over Noah's body. She cradled his head in her lap. His eyes were closed. She could smell blood. "Noah, are you okay? Please tell me you're okay!"

His eyelids fluttered, and he groaned. Slowly he sat up holding his injured arm. "Aw, Doc, still worrying about your patient? I'm fine." He smiled at her, showing off his cute dimple.

Talia released the breath she'd pent up. He was alive. She could slap him for scaring her like that, but instead she helped him to his feet as men and women in FBI jackets and police uniforms approached.

A man in tactical gear came up to them. "You Noah Landers and Talia Knowles?"

Noah stepped in front of her. Ever the protector. "Yes. Nice timing."

"I'm Agent Sims, a friend of Justin's. You okay?"

Noah shook the man's hand. "Yeah, I'm fine."

What? She stomped over to the two. "No, he's not fine. He opened his gunshot wound. Do you have a medical team that can help?"

"Talia, I'm—"

She rounded on Noah, poking him in the chest with

her finger. "Don't say 'fine.' That's a lie. You're not fine. Look how much you're bleeding."

Sims coughed but might've been covering up a laugh. "Come with me. We'll get you some medical attention, and then we'll need a statement from you both."

Not sure what was so funny about reopening a gunshot wound, but if he brought them to medical professionals, she'd let it slide.

He led the way out of the hangar. "Any idea who these guys are?" he asked as they skirted the two wounded and cuffed men and out to an ambulance in the museum parking lot.

A chilly breeze blew when they stepped into the open area. Talia pulled her vest tighter around her. "No clue. They didn't use names except for Kim. They kidnapped Sally, my…aunt yesterday. I think she was in the jet that took off right before you arrived. And somehow, they were tracking us. Or at least me."

Simms nodded. "Probably your cell phones. Hand them to me. I'll have our tech guy check them out."

A paramedic took over from there, checking Noah's vitals and wound. "Yup, looks like you ripped it open again. Gonna have to take you in."

"We don't have time to go to the emergency room. Can you just patch it up best you can?"

The medic shook her head. "I can bandage it, but I can't do any suturing. It would be better for you to get this stitched up."

"Bandages will be fine."

Humph. And he called *her* stubborn?

Once the paramedic was finished, Noah retrieved his hat from behind the hangar, and Agent Sims and another FBI agent took their statements. "Alright, I'm going to need that drone footage. FBI will take over the case now that we've established it crosses state lines. These two guys are from California."

California? Was that where they took Sally? "Do you know that jet's destination?"

Sims looked down over his notes. "Flight plan said a small airport outside of Seattle, but the control deck said they didn't head that way."

Noah sighed. "So we have no clue where they took Sally."

"Are you sure she was in the jet?" the other agent asked.

Talia spoke up. "I didn't see her. But they talked about the old lady being kept in there. One of the guys had a girlfriend or something in the hangar. She wasn't old, though. She threw a fit like a little kid when they told her to get on the plane. She screamed when he picked her up and carried her into the jet himself. So I assume the old lady they were talking about is Sally."

"And any idea why they're determined to find you?"

"I told you about the only threats I could think of. But this seems a little extreme for that kind of grudge."

Sims stopped taking notes and closed his little book. "You two should come with us. We can find you a safe place to wait this out."

This again? "I want to help find Sally."

"You've seen how dangerous that can be. These people mean business. If we hadn't arrived when we did, you would be dead. We've got this under control."

Really? People kept saying that, but it didn't seem like they were any closer to knowing who wanted her dead. The complete *lack* of control or answers had her terrified. But she couldn't sit around and wait. She needed to do something. "I want to help."

"I get that. But the best thing you can do now is lay low. Stay safe."

"Then I'll stay at the ranch. We can see anyone coming into the valley. I don't want to sit around an office."

The agent stared for a beat. Then he dug into his pocket and held a white rectangle out to her. "Here's my card. Call me if you think of anything else."

With a curt nod, she turned and walked back to the car. She didn't want the agent to see the tears that escaped and rolled down her cheeks. She swiped them away. She'd failed Sally. And now, when she had way more questions and secrets than answers, she needed her more than ever. Sally had been her rock. The one constant in her life. So many things she thought were true were lies. The uncertainty of it all threatened to cave in on her. She might sound tough, but now, in the quiet of the car, fatigue swept through her. Tremors shook her.

Noah slipped into the passenger seat. "What do we do now?"

Good question with no good answer.

Noah rubbed his hands together to warm them up. At least in the car they were out of the wind. The bullet he'd dodged was a close call. And the reality of it was hitting hard. The shaking inside said he might not be as "fine" as he thought. But no need to admit that to Talia or the paramedic. The shakes would wear off soon. Hopefully.

He looked over at Talia sitting in the driver's seat of her neighbor's car. She probably wouldn't like him knowing it, but he caught her swiping a tear or two from her eyes. She wouldn't look at him either. Time to break out the charm.

"Well, little lady, I was hopin' you'd have a brilliant idea to crack the case," he said in his best John Wayne impression.

She looked at him like he'd lost his mind, but at least she was making eye contact again. "Why are you talking like that?"

He laughed. "I was just trying to cheer you up."

"Well, I don't need cheering up. I need ideas. We have no clue where that plane is heading, where Sally is, or who's trying to kill me."

"Yeah. That's not much to go on." Silence filled the car. Noah stared out at the hills, wishing he had more to give her.

"Noah, what's something my father would do in a situation like this?"

"Your dad?" So many memories of Doug Coleson, his laugh when they played family charades at the ranch, his quiet thinking face when he helped them with their model rockets, and other moments from the past all rushed through his mind. One snagged his attention. "I remember once when Xander and I were on one of those camping trips. He let us hike a shorter trail alone. He told us if we got lost, to retrace our steps and go back to the beginning. Maybe that's what we should do."

"Go back to the beginning?"

He nodded. Of course! He should've thought of it sooner. "We can go back to Sally's ranch. You can check on Peaches and the other animals, and we could see if she left any other clues. Maybe she knows more about what's going on and why."

Determination replaced the hopelessness that filled

Talia's eyes. "Yes. That sounds reasonable. Everyone in the hangar was on that plane or in custody."

"Before we go, we should see if there's anything else they could be tracking us through. And we'll have to get some new phones since the FBI has ours."

They opened the doors and searched the car, the wheel wells, the bumpers, inside under the rugs, everything for any sign of a tracking device.

Noah closed the trunk and leaned against the vehicle. "We didn't have much when we ran. I don't even know how they would have gotten a tracker on the car when we didn't even know we'd be using it."

"Like the agent said, it was probably our phones they were tracking." Talia picked up Sunny in the back seat and checked the mats on the floor and the seats. He tried the front seats. Nothing.

Talia moved to the driver's seat and started the engine.

No use fighting over who was driving this time. With his arm screaming at him like it was, she could take the wheel. He needed all the energy he could conserve. This battle was far from over. "Let's get back to Mustang Sally Ranch and see if we can find some more answers."

Talia's fingers, currently wrapped around the steering wheel of the car, itched to feel Peaches, to tangle them in her mane and to see for herself that she was okay.

Some might think animals didn't care, but Peaches understood her. The horse always picked up when she was upset or excited. It was as if Peaches absorbed the nervous energy and would release it bit by bit as they rode together. And right now, "upset" didn't even begin to describe her state of being.

Yes, a ride would help clear her head, move past all the feelings she couldn't name or understand, feelings that were clogging up her thinking. If she could just saddle up her horse and ride, she could figure all this out.

Sally had put off Talia's questions for a long while. But now was the time for answers, even if Talia didn't like them. Even if they displaced her sense of security. She was still recovering from the shock of Sally not being her aunt or related to her in any way. And something told her there were a lot more earth-shattering revelations coming.

"Noah." She took a deep breath and let it out in a rush before she could lose all courage. "How did my family die?"

"You don't know?" His voice was low, quiet.

"Sally told me they died in a car accident, but I'm finding myself questioning everything she told me about them, especially after what you said about your father."

Silence. "Are you sure…?"

"I appreciate you want to spare me the pain, but twenty-five years is a long time to wait. It's time I learned the truth."

He sighed, took off his hat and started fiddling with the band. "It was a week after your fourth birthday. One Saturday we were celebrating with ponies on your back lawn, and the next Saturday they were gone."

"What happened?"

"There was an explosion. In your home. Actually, multiple explosions, bombs strategically placed so the whole mansion fell. A gang called the East Fourteenth Street gang was responsible. But officials said everyone would've died instantly in the blast, so at least you can know they didn't suffer."

Echoes of loud booms and fire. Her breathing sped up. Nausea rose inside.

"How did Sally and I escape?" She managed to get the words out, but her throat was closing up.

"No one knows but Sally. We only knew that they never found your body or hers in the rubble."

"Why? Why did this gang hate us so much?"

"The police couldn't find a direct motive, so they speculate that the gang was hired. It's been a big mystery. That and your disappearance. And later, officials found accounts in my father's name with deposits from a known gang member. The media said he was working with them, but nothing was ever proven." Noah's voice faded. "Talia? You okay?"

She nodded, but she wasn't okay.

Noah grabbed the wheel as she drifted toward the edge of the road. "Hey there. Why don't you pull over for a second? This is a lot to take in."

His voice barely registered, but he was right. She pulled over to the side of the road and ran out to the sagebrush, leaving her door wide open and the engine running.

The smell of acrid smoke and dust. Loud noises. Noises that shook the earth. She covered her ears.

She curled up, sitting on cold ground, burying her head in her arms, knees pulled in.

So loud. The booms were so loud. And screaming. She remembered hearing screaming. Heat, choking ash, and shrill screams in the night. Her ears felt like they would burst. She was lost in the deafening noise and couldn't find her way out.

And then a warmth overtook her. A steady rhythm broke through the chaos in her head.

Noah.

He held her. It was his heartbeat she heard, slowly drawing her out of the horrific place her mind went to.

He whispered into her hair. "Hey, it's okay. I'm here."

She looked up at him. "I think I remember it."

"I'm so sorry."

She wept. She held on to him and cried like she had never cried before. Buried somewhere deep inside, her four-year-old self remembered and was finally allowed to release the grief.

Noah held her for a long time. The sun was high overhead and moving west in the vast blue sky. They sat in the middle of the desert, no one around. A screech of a hawk circling above and then a quiet breeze rustling the bushes were the only sounds. That and the sobs absorbed by his shirt as he cradled Talia's head on his chest.

She was remembering.

Maybe this was what Sally was afraid of. That the overwhelming grief would break her.

It was like she was crumbling in his hands. His heart broke for her.

But the crying eventually subsided. She shuddered and lifted her head, her blue eyes red and swollen, full of anguish. She sniffed. "I think I remember the explosion. I can't see it, but I remember hearing big booms and smelling fire. I remember running and screaming."

He could only nod.

She stood and wiped her cheeks, streaked with dirt and tears. "And it makes so much sense now. I hate the Fourth of July. I can't stand the fireworks, the loud noise they make. I always wondered why. Now I know."

Without a word, they started making their way back

to the car side by side. She stopped. "Wait. Your father. You said he died in an explosion."

"The same explosion. My father worked for your family. He was the head of security for them."

She stepped closer to him, closer than she should, and faced him. "And people think he helped this gang?"

Noah took a step back. Here it came. The judgment. The hatred. He braced himself. "Yes."

But Talia's eyes were clear. She didn't step away in horror or as if she was afraid of being tainted by him. "What do you think?"

"I don't know." He stumbled over the words. There was a lot more to it than that. "I mean, our parents were best friends. I could never imagine my dad doing something like that. He was my hero as a kid. But then the papers, the media, they tore him to shreds. There was no proof and a lot of speculation, but…no one really knows."

Best case scenario, his father failed to keep them safe. Just like he failed Kelley. "Talia, my mom refuses to believe any of the allegations. My father loved your family. We were all close friends. He would always tell me it wasn't just his job to keep you safe. It was his honor."

Noah told himself that line about honor, but inside he doubted. He couldn't shake the shame of a disgraced name. He thought it would be better when he legally switched his name to Landers to escape the association with the man he'd idolized as a child. Henry Dillard.

But what did a kid really know? And the truth was, his mother didn't know either. Her blind faith in the man was still as strong today as it was twenty-five years ago.

The police couldn't question a dead man about suspicious deposits. But it sealed his father's guilt as far as the public was concerned. Noah didn't know who to believe.

The commercial asking for help finding Anna Coleson might have prompted Noah to find Gregory's niece, but the truth was, Noah was already looking. Looking for Carol and Anna and looking for answers. Gregory's request and generous offer to breed his racehorse with Excalibur just gave him the means to follow his heart. "Talia, if you remembered the explosion, do you remember anything about my father? Henry?"

Her face was unreadable. "No. I don't remember anything about him."

Then Sally was their last hope of knowing anything more about how the Colesons died. They needed to find her soon. And he should find someone else to keep Talia safe. He obviously wasn't doing a great job of it.

NINE

She shouldn't let Noah drive with an injured arm, but Talia could hardly lift her head, let alone her own arms to hold a steering wheel. Her legs felt like lead, and her head pounded. They weren't too far now. She closed her eyes and hummed. She drifted off to a dreamless sleep to the quiet country music station Noah found.

She woke with a start when the car slowed to a crawl. Her eyes opened to a familiar sight, and newfound energy pumped through her veins. This wasn't the Mustang Sally Ranch. But it was even better for what she needed right now. A friend.

As soon as Noah parked the car at the Jordan Creek Ranch house, Talia burst out of the passenger seat and ran to the barn.

Peaches!

It was only a little more than twenty-four hours' separation, but with everything that happened, it felt like months. Talia buried her nose in the palomino's mane, breathing in the scent of horse and leather. "Hey girl. I'm here."

Peaches huffed.

"I know. We didn't find her. But we will. We have

to." Talia stroked Peaches's forehead and was rewarded with a nuzzle of her wet snout.

"Talia? That you?"

Beau Polecheski came down the aisle of the barn toward her.

"Yeah, it's me. Just had to check on my girl."

"She's been a good guest. Any news on Sally?"

"No. But we're still looking."

"So strange, all this happening in the middle of our valley. Sally Knowles is tough, but she's good people. Can't imagine anyone wanting to hurt her."

Talia could only nod as she continued to stroke her horse.

"Is it something in her past coming back to haunt her?"

"I… I'm not really sure."

"Why don't you come on up to the house. Alice is getting an early supper together. We'll eat in an hour, but you can come visit for a bit."

Talia moved to grab a saddle blanket. "No, thank you."

Noah walked into the barn. A smile that crinkled his eyes and showed off his dimple took her breath away. She was never one to be boy-crazy or drool over a handsome man. But this cowboy? She couldn't account for the way he made her feel.

And that was dangerous. She needed time away from him. "Noah, why don't you meet me back at the ranch? I'll ride Peaches there."

Yes, some time away from Noah's enigmatic presence was what she needed if she was going to sort anything out.

Noah stepped up and took the blanket from her hand.

"No way. I know all you want to do is hop on her and ride. That's why I came here first. But we better get back to Sally's and see what we can find."

"I need to ride." She stared him down, then Beau.

Noah met her stare with steel in his own. He took a broad stance in front of her and crossed his arms, his military background evident. "No, you need to be safe."

"But I *am* safe when I'm out there!" Didn't they get it? Riding was her safe place. She was in control. Everything made sense. No one teased her out there. No one gave her strange looks because she goofed up some unwritten social cue. She didn't have to remember to look people in the eye, watch her fidgeting hands, or fight the constant drive to rock on her heels. On horseback she knew exactly what to do and felt capable enough to do it. She could sort through all the tangled feelings and think straight.

And there was way too much feeling going on inside her, and not enough sense.

Beau walked away from the tense atmosphere filling the barn.

Noah stomped over to the rack and threw the blanket down. "Talia, you might not care about your own safety, but I do! There are people out there trying to kill you. We need answers. I get that you want to run away from it all on the back of your mare, but that's not going to help us find Sally."

Run away from it all. Is that what she was doing? Maybe. Maybe that's exactly what she'd been doing all these years.

She stilled. "It's not that I don't care about the danger or Sally. I just… I just wanted a few minutes when things didn't seem to be spinning so far out of control."

A heavy sigh deflated Noah's stiff shoulders. His voice softened. "I know. And I get that. There's nothing better than a full-out gallop in the wide-open spaces when you've got a lot on your mind. But riding out there in the wilderness will put you and your horse at more risk. Let's keep Peaches here where she's safe and head back to Sally's ranch."

She couldn't refute his logic, and somehow it helped that he seemed to understand. It was time to do a little growing up and face the hard stuff. Peaches would still be here when all of this was over. With one last nuzzle and heavy steps, Talia followed Noah to the car, and they went back to where this awful nightmare had begun. Mustang Sally Ranch.

Noah bypassed the bloodstain on the ground once more and walked up the porch steps to Sally's empty house while Talia went to check on the animals in the barn. It was eerily quiet in the yard. Even the wind chimes hung limp and silent. Inside wasn't much better. The mess was still on the dining room table. The air stale. He went through and opened windows to let in fresh air.

He should try to track down more leads while waiting for Talia. It was plain to see they both needed a little space. He couldn't let her ride off to the wild blue yonder, but he could give her a few minutes in the barn. And he wouldn't mind a little time to get his own emotions under control and stuffed back in the deepest recesses of his soul. The more he was with the woman, the more he wanted to spend time with her.

He wanted to be the one to hold her when she was upset, ride with her in the wilds of the Owyhees and see the smile that she kept hidden so well. He was in as much danger as she was.

He shook off the stubborn dreams of long rides with Talia and sat down to Sally's laptop at the table. The only thing he could think of to look up was Dwight Quincy, the manager Talia reported for abusing the mustangs.

A basic search showed he was originally from the Pocatello area. Looked like his family in eastern Idaho had money. Quincy Farms & Foods was one of the major employers in that area, with a potato processing plant and acres and acres of fields. At some point he moved to Boise and managed one of the mustang holding facilities outside of the city.

The state's Bureau of Land Management's website must not have been updated often. It still listed him as the contact and site manager for wild horse and burro adoptions. Talia said he had been fired. But maybe he could dig a little.

Noah dialed the office number for Dwight. A woman answered.

"Hi, I'm looking for Dwight Quincy."

"Sorry. He's no longer at this office."

"Oh, he got a better offer, huh? Figured he would move up the ranks quickly."

"Up the ranks? No. Dwight was fired."

"That's too bad. Um, do you have a way I could reach him? I might have a job for him if he's looking."

"Unless you're the governor, he won't care."

"The governor?"

"He won't give you the time of day unless you're with the state. He's had his eye on a spot in the Department of Agriculture."

"Well, I'd still like to catch up with him. Do you have a phone number for him?"

"Nope."

"Forwarding address?"

"Look, you sound nice, so I'll give you a little advice when it comes to Mr. Quincy. Don't waste your time on this guy. I worked for him for the last five years, and he still couldn't remember my first name when he left. So no, he didn't give me his personal phone number on his way out, and I was fine with that."

"Okay. Thanks for your help."

Political aspirations, sounded like a jerk and one with plenty of money. But was he willing to hire goons to kidnap Sally and shoot up Talia's house?

He should write these questions down and discuss them with Talia when she returned. He picked up the pen and notebook Sally left there with her "key = mustang" on the top page. He turned to a fresh sheet, but the pen wouldn't work. After fiddling with it for a minute he searched the house for another one.

There. On a little table by the recliner in the living room, he spotted a Bible and pen. He reached for the pen but knocked the Bible to the rug. The soft cover was tattered and worn, the pages filled with highlighted and underlined verses, notes in the margins. Like Talia's stuffed horse, this book was well-loved. He picked it up and set it on the table. He was about to walk away with the pen in hand when he saw the photo lying on the rug. Must've fallen out of the Bible.

It was yellowed, had that vintage look. It was folded to show a young girl and boy wearing bell-bottoms. When opened flat on the other side of the fold, two men wore thick mustaches with big glasses. Definitely from the seventies. It wasn't the Colesons, so it must have been from Sally's past.

Spidery script on the back read Rodrigo, Carolina, y Pablo con Sebastian. La Casa de Los Vasquez. Caracas, Venezuela.

Talia walked in. "What's that?"

"I think it's a picture of Carol."

She rushed over and took the picture out of his hand, studied it. "Yes. That's Carol. Look at the birthmark on the girl's arm. Sally has the same one. Who are these other people?"

"It kind of looks like this might be her brother, and maybe one of the men is her father? Let's see what we can find out." A quick search on the computer for Vasquez in Caracas Venezuela came up with a ton of hits, but the top ones all included a Vasquez drug cartel in the title.

Noah's mouth went dry. A drug cartel?

Talia looked over his shoulder. Her voice shook as she whispered, "Do you think Sally was from a drug cartel family?"

He took out the burner phone they'd purchased on the way and snapped a photo of the picture front and back. A possible scenario spun through his mind. "Say Carol grew up and escaped from her drug-running family, became a nanny for your family. The Vasquez cartel discovered her and blew up your mansion as revenge, only to discover later that she escaped."

"Why would they want me, then?" Talia's eyes narrowed.

Noah stood and faced her. Finally pieces were coming together to make sense. It was the traction they needed. "Don't you see? You're the only person she cares about in the world. They might want you to hurt her."

"I don't know—"

"Talia, this would explain why you moved so much. She was running from them and protecting you."

"But would this Vasquez cartel from South America work with a California Asian gang? All the men at the hanger were of Asian descent."

Her question stalled him for a moment until he remembered something. "The East Fourteenth gang were Asian, yes, but they were also heavy into the drug trade and arms, so maybe there was a connection. Maybe the Vasquezes are their supplier?"

Talia plopped down on the chair. "That's still a lot of assumptions."

"Yeah, but doesn't it make sense?"

"Maybe. But we need facts. Not speculation."

They were getting closer. Noah could feel it. "Sally would have at least some of the answers."

And they needed to find her before she disappeared with them.

TEN

Talia stared at the notepad on the table again, trying to make sense of it all. Sally/Carol possibly from a drug cartel. Her nanny-turned-aunt.

Was anything she knew true anymore? How many secrets were still to be revealed? According to the online articles they skimmed about the Vasquez Cartel, if these were the people after her, they had plenty of cruelty and means.

She shivered.

Noah moved to the living room and sent a picture of the photo to Justin. He slipped the phone back in his pocket and stared at the other photos on a shelf. For some strange reason, she wanted to be closer to him. It was warmer near Noah, safer.

But before she could join him, he rushed over carrying a frame. "Tal, did you see this? Where is this taken?"

She looked down at the familiar picture of her standing out in the bluffs with Pixie, a painted mare she had in high school. "That's just an old junk pile, out on the trail. Used to be a bunk house and shed out there at one point when this ranch was a bigger operation, long before we moved here. The rancher here before us parked his old trucks and cars out there, and we bought the place as-is."

"Yeah, but look at this."

He pointed to the only car she and Sally had brought with them. "That thing is so old, it barely made it out here when we moved to the ranch. Had it forever, though. Sally parked it out there thinking we'd get it fixed up someday."

He looked at her like she was missing something. Something obvious. He shook his head. "Don't you know what kind of car that is?"

"We just called it the convertible. Now that I think about it, it was kind of impractical for a car. But I never questioned how we got around."

"Talia, it's a Mustang."

"So?" Why couldn't he just spit it out? She felt more stupid by the second.

"The 'key equals mustang.' This was your *dad's* old Mustang."

Mustang?

Oh!

They both rushed to the door. Noah opened it for her. "How far away is it?"

"A mile or two. I always lose track of time when I ride out there, so I'm not sure." They stood on the porch, darkness starting to creep up the eastern horizon.

"It will be dark soon. What's the fastest way to get there? Horseback?"

"Zeus is the only horse here that could be ridden, but he's ornery. He only responds to Sally. The others are all mustangs that haven't been trained yet. We could take the ATV."

Talia led him to the shed with the four-wheeler. More

awake than she'd been all day, she was finally doing something productive. They grabbed water canteens, flashlights, and hopped on. Noah told her to drive so he could watch their back and probably to rest his arm. He still had his gun, holstered under his jacket.

He scanned the hills as she started the engine. "I don't like being exposed like this, so let's do this as fast as we can and get back."

Thankful to be out in the fresh air, even though she wasn't riding Peaches, Talia drove them out to the old bunkhouse/car graveyard. The trail was quiet but bumpy. Every now and then, Noah's arm tightened around her, sending little spurts of energy through her. Somehow his touch was equal parts exhilarating and calming. She was almost sorry when they reached the cars.

Many of the rusted vehicles were here before they bought the place and weren't worth the money to haul away. A tumbleweed rolled past them and out toward the sunset as they got off the ATV and started searching the black Mustang convertible.

Talia started with the glove box, shining her flashlight on the papers in it. "What are we looking for?"

"Some kind of key. Or a clue. I don't know exactly. Hopefully we'll know it when we see it." Noah fiddled with the knobs and steering wheel.

"Well, the keys would be in the visor."

He flipped it down, and the keys fell into his hand. "We'll bring these with us, but let's keep looking in case it's not something so obvious."

After a thorough search of the interior and trunk, they came up with a long-lost braided leather keychain, wrappers from Sally's favorite brand of gum, an old CD, and eighty-two cents in change.

Get ready to relax and indulge with your **FREE BOOKS** and more!

Claim up to FOUR NEW BOOKS & TWO MYSTERY GIFTS – absolutely FREE!

Dear Reader,

We both know life can be difficult at times. That's why it's important to treat yourself so you can relax and recharge once in a while.

And I'd like to help you do this by sending you this amazing offer of up to FOUR brand new full length FREE BOOKS that WE pay for.

This is everything I have ready to send to you right now:

Try **Love Inspired® Romance Larger-Print** books and fall in love with inspirational romances that take you on an uplifting journey of faith, forgiveness and hope.

Try **Love Inspired® Suspense Larger-Print** books where courage and optimism unite in stories of faith and love in the face of danger.

Or **TRY BOTH!**

All we ask in return is that you answer 4 simple questions on the attached Treat Yourself survey. You'll get **Two Free Books** and **Two Mystery Gifts** from each series you try, *altogether worth over $20!* Who could pass up a deal like that?

Sincerely,

Pam Powers

Harlequin Reader Service

Treat Yourself to Free Books and Free Gifts.

Answer 4 fun questions and get rewarded.

We love to connect with our readers! Please tell us a little about you...

	YES	NO
1. I LOVE reading a good book.	◯	◯
2. I indulge and "treat" myself often.	◯	◯
3. I love getting FREE things.	◯	◯
4. Reading is one of my favorite activities.	◯	◯

▶ DETACH AND MAIL CARD TODAY! ▶

TREAT YOURSELF • Pick your 2 Free Books...

Yes! Please send me my Free Books from each series I select and Free Mystery Gifts. I understand that I am under no obligation to buy anything, as explained on the back of this card.

Which do you prefer?

❏ **Love Inspired® Romance Larger-Print** 122/322 IDL GRDP
❏ **Love Inspired® Suspense Larger-Print** 107/307 IDL GRDP
❏ **Try Both** 122/322 & 107/307 IDL GRED

FIRST NAME

LAST NAME

ADDRESS

APT.#

CITY

STATE/PROV.

ZIP/POSTAL CODE

EMAIL ❏ Please check this box if you would like to receive newsletters and promotional emails from Harlequin Enterprises ULC and its affiliates. You can unsubscribe anytime.

© 2022 HARLEQUIN ENTERPRISES ULC
™ and ® are trademarks owned by Harlequin Enterprises ULC. Printed in the U.S.A.

LI/SLI-520-TY22

school, I got to know one girl and was so excited to be invited to her birthday party. But when the girls started playing stupid kissing games with the boys in Rachel Lowe's basement, I was uncomfortable. I snuck out to the backyard. They had a gorgeous collie. And I wanted to try to communicate with it. To study the dog, I copied its behaviors. So, I got down on all fours and mimicked canine vocalization—"

"You barked?"

"Yes. And then the rest of the kids saw me there and thought it was hilarious. Called me Dog-face the rest of the time we were there. The boys would bark whenever they saw me. Rachel said she only befriended me as a joke and never let me forget it. I was actually glad to leave that school. But the lesson always stayed with me. I would never fit in."

"Kids can be so mean." His own memories came back to mind.

"What do you know about mean kids?"

"Plenty."

"But you're friendly. Good-looking. What would anybody tease you about?"

"Kids will find something to pick on. I had a lot of friends one day. The next they turned their backs on me and mocked me, said I was just like my dad. They hated him for betraying your family." He kicked a small stone in their path. "But they were wrong, Talia. You do have a place you fit in. And you don't need to change who you are to please anybody. You were smart to leave that Danny guy, because you deserve so much better."

"Part of me really just wanted to have kids so I could have more family, you know? But maybe I'm the end of the Coleson line, and maybe that's okay. I just...now I just want to make them proud."

Noah swallowed hard. She wasn't the end of the Colesons. She was strong enough, no matter what Sally thought. Maybe it was time they talked to Gregory and asked for his help. It was time for her to meet her uncle.

"Talia, you're—"

She gasped as she stopped in the middle of the trail and pointed. "What's that?"

Something bright was lighting up the sky ahead, something in the direction of the ranch. They ran ahead to the bend in the trail and skidded to a stop.

The ranch house and barn were engulfed in flames.

ELEVEN

Talia ran toward her burning home. The house was already a pile of rubble and blaze. The barn still stood, but it glowed with unholy light. The windows and door in the front of the building belched orange plumes and ghostly gray smoke, turning the structure into a hulking dragon shooting out its deadly flames into the night.

"The animals!" She had to save them.

"Talia, stop! It might be a trap!" Noah ran up to her and grabbed her arm, tugging her back.

"I can't let them burn!" She shoved against his rock-solid hold. "Let me go!"

"You need to be safe. Wait here."

They were close enough to hear the roar and crackle of the fire. The bleating of one of the goats. It sounded scared.

"Noah, I have to get to them. I have to—"

He pulled her into a tight embrace and spoke into her ear. His voice was strong enough to penetrate the terror. "Talia, stay here. Someone is trying to kill you. Help by calling 911. I'll save the animals."

"No—"

He slapped his phone into her hand and ran toward the barn before she could say more.

Lord, why is this happening?

Watching the flames lick the walls of the barn, and what had once been the house, sparks flying up into the now black night sky, her prayer rose as her heart was breaking.

This was the first place she and Sally had that felt like home. She enjoyed her little cottage in Orchard Springs, but this ranch saved her. She found the solace she needed to heal from so many moves and all the issues at school. She found peace with being herself. She dug into her passion for horses and animals. It all happened here. And it was turning to fire and ash before her eyes.

Noah reached the fire, his silhouette black against the bright yellow-and-orange inferno. He ran toward the corral at the back of the barn and opened the gate, shooing the cows out to safety. He must've found a way into the building and opened the stalls, because soon the three mustangs ran out. But where was Zeus? Talia started to run.

Come on, Noah. Get Zeus and get out of there!

A crash of something falling sent a flurry of sparks and smoke out the roof and the hayloft window.

"Noah!"

Talia reached the edge of the barnyard. Noah's phone in her hand buzzed with an incoming text message.

The phone. Right. She was supposed to call for help.

She dialed 911. "This is Talia Knowles. I'm at Mustang Sally Ranch on Red Canyon Road. The house and barn are on fire. Hurry!" She sprinted to the barn in a frantic rush. A wall of intense heat bore down on her as she approached the main opening. She stopped in her tracks, flung her hands up to shield her face against the bellowing fire. "Noah!"

A chicken squawked and rushed out the open barn door, the only thing small enough to sneak under the flames that swallowed the frame and door post. No sign of Noah.

She ran around the back. The back door that led to the corral was open. The fire hadn't reached it yet. She jumped over the corral fence and stepped into the burning building, choking on the thick smoke, straining to see as her eyes watered and burned. Where was he?

There. Through the haze, she could see his outline. She moved closer. Noah held his shirt over his nose with one hand. The other tugged on Zeus's halter, trying to get the massive horse to move. The blaze behind Noah crawled closer. Menacing flames danced along the ridgepole above them.

"Noah, come on!" She had to yell to be heard above the cry of the fire.

"I can't get him to move!"

Zeus rose up on his hind legs and neighed. Talia tried to grab hold of the halter too, but Zeus flung his head back and forth.

A section of roof fell and landed on the hay in the next stall, the hungry fire now between them and the door.

"Talia, we have to go! That's going to cut off our only exit!"

"Zeus!" She lunged once more for his halter and caught the lead rope. She pulled with all her weight. Noah grabbed it too and leaned back. Her hands blistered as she strained, sliding against the line.

But Zeus refused to be led. The horse wouldn't move

out of his stall. He reared up once more and kicked. Noah and Talia's hands slid to the end of the rope. Zeus stomped. Noah cried out in pain as a hoof landed on his boot. He dropped the rope and fell back. Talia let go and dragged Noah away from the panicked horse, who finally bolted out of his stall, leaped over the fire devouring the straw on the floor, and ran out the corral door.

The fire snaked closer to them. Noah stood and dropped his shirt. "We have to g—" His words cut off with a fit of coughing.

She nodded, smoke burning her eyes. She grabbed his arm and threw it over her shoulder, letting him use her as a crutch as he hopped on one foot to the door.

They gulped fresh air as soon as they cleared the barn. Noah didn't stop for long though. He limped to the nearest horse trough and grabbed the bucket. He scooped water and flung it at the burning barn wall. Talia spun around, looking for another bucket. Instead she spied the hose and ran to the outdoor pump and turned it on.

She aimed the water at the corral opening where the fire leaped and licked up the dry hay on the ground and the frame of the door.

Noah continued to fling water.

The fire kept growing, roaring out of control.

Her hose water only created more steam and smoke.

Suddenly a loud creak rang out. The ridgepole down the middle of the barn shuddered. Crashed down. The roof collapsed with a burst of flames shooting up into the sky. The dragon screaming in victory.

"No!" Talia dropped her hose and fell to her knees in the mud. Noah was there in a second, strong arms around her, pulling into his chest. And she fell apart once again.

* * *

If Noah never stepped foot in a hospital ever again, it would be alright with him. The smell, the shrill beeping of alarms and machines, the lighting…he hated everything about them. If they hadn't cut off his jeans and boot last night to get to his injured foot, he'd be out of here. But it was a little cold to walk out of the Boise hospital barefoot in his boxers and a T-shirt.

Of course, he wouldn't be walking, not with the damage Zeus did to his foot. The horse rendered his foot useless, unable to bear any weight for at least a few weeks while the bones healed.

No, he wouldn't be getting out of here without crutches and a surgical boot. Just add it to the humiliation and mounting hospital bills he *did* bear.

He had plenty of those to last a lifetime too.

His mother's bout with cancer five years ago was finally paid off after taking out the second mortgage on the ranch. The mortgage they couldn't now pay without Gregory's help.

And what would Sally and Talia do?

Last night's events tore through his mind. Alice, Beau and the whole crew showed up just as the barn roof caved in. The fire department did what they could, but neither the house nor the barn was salvageable. The car in the driveway they borrowed from Talia's neighbor and a few outbuildings were the only things to survive at the Mustang Sally Ranch. The Polecheskis helped round up the animals they were able to capture and put up temporary stockades. Ed, one of the other hands at Jordan Creek, brought Noah to the ER while Talia treated the animals that were injured.

He should've been out there helping her. He should've

done a lot of things. But his failures at keeping her safe kept piling up.

He released a sigh, but it didn't relieve the tension across his shoulders. Now he was tied down with an IV line, an oxygen sensor, a wicked cough, and enough shame to bury him for good.

A soft knock on the door interrupted his pity party. "It's Talia. Can I come in?"

"Yeah." He sat up a little straighter, gritting his teeth when the movement sent a bolt of pain up his leg. His sharp intake of breath sent him into a coughing spasm.

She slid the curtains back and came up to his bedside. "That doesn't sound good. How are you doing?" Instead of looking at him, she studied the numbers on the screens as if the answer she was looking for was on them.

She must've had a shower at Jordan Creek Ranch. Face fresh, clean hair, only a hint of smoke, but tired, tired eyes. Eyes that wouldn't meet his.

"I'm okay. How's Zeus?"

She sniffed. "His lungs need time to recover, and he's more ornery than ever, but he'll make it."

"Did the fire department know what started the fires?"

"I haven't heard yet." She barely looked him in the eye. She rocked on her heels and went back to studying the screens.

Something was wrong. Something she didn't want to tell him.

"Talia, what is it?"

"Your numbers look good. I'm not a medical doctor, of course, but—"

"Hey." He tapped her hand that rested on his bed rail.

"What's going on in that head of yours? Well, besides the obvious grief from losing your home and Sally kidnapped."

She gave him a half smile. "Besides that?" She dropped into the chair by his bed and finally looked at him. "You almost died in that fire."

"But I didn't. I'm here. And as soon as the doc clears me—and Ed brings me some clothes—we'll be out of here and back on the case. We'll find Sally."

"Noah, you almost died. You've been shot, almost run off the road, and now the fire. You should get as far away from me as possible."

"I'm not going anywhere."

"But I'm not good for you. I bring danger and heartbreak."

Okay, now he was really confused. "What are you talking about?"

She sighed and leaned closer to him. "On the one hand, I want you to stay and help. You're the first person in a long time who I trust. Who gets me at least a little bit. But around me you've been shot, on the run, burned, suffered from smoke inhalation and stomped on by a horse. I think you should go back home and heal. I should find Sally alone."

"Talia, you're not alone."

She bolted out of her chair. "But maybe I should be!" She paced along his bedside. He grunted when he reached out for her and was held back by his IV line. She was like a wounded animal crawling back and forth in a cage. She needed to be set free. She needed to know the truth. Whether Sally thought so or not, it was time she knew that she wasn't alone.

Noah ripped out his IV line and the sensors on his

chest. The machines immediately started beeping. Talia rushed to him. "What are you doing? You can't take that line out!" She grabbed a wad of tissues and pressed it against his hand where it was bleeding.

He reached over with the other hand and turned off the machine monitoring his heart rate and oxygen levels. "Hey. I need to tell you something. I tried to tell you sooner, and every time I did something—"

"Noah, you need to get this line back in. Where's the nurse?"

"Talia, I don't need a nurse. I need you to listen."

She kept examining his hand and the port he'd just ripped out. "We need to keep you hydrated and—"

He pulled his hand out of her reach. She frowned and grabbed for it again, focused on the wrong thing.

"Talia, stop."

"This is serious." She reached again for his hand but missed. "Forget it. Where's the call button? I'll get the nurse back in here."

"You're not the only Coleson alive!"

Her face went pale as she dropped the tissues. "What did you say?"

He had her attention. "You have an uncle. Gregory Coleson. And he's searching for you. That's the real reason I was looking for you. Well, that and I was hoping to talk to Sally about the last time she saw my dad. I wanted to tell you about it all earlier, but…"

His voice trailed off as he studied her. Her face went blank. He couldn't tell if she was angry or scared, or shocked.

Finally, she blinked. "An uncle? I have an uncle?"

"Yes. He's your dad's brother. They were in business together. He lives near San Jose, where he still runs the

Coleson Company. He's not married. Never had any children. You're the only family he has left. And he's been searching for you since you disappeared."

"Why…why didn't I know this?"

"Sally was trying to protect you. She said she never knew who to trust after your family was killed. When I found her, the day before you and I met, I told her that Gregory Coleson was looking for you. I wanted to bring you to him. But Sally was scared. Scared for you. She wanted to be the one to tell you. Said that you'd need a little more time to take it all in and process it before we could go meet him. But she was kidnapped before she could talk to you."

"Kidnapped before—" her hand slapped down on the bedside tray, a glower on her face. "She had over twenty-five years to tell me!"

There was no question now as to how she was feeling. Fury snapped in her eyes.

"Look, I'm not going to say what Sally did was right or wrong, but I do think she did what she did to keep you safe."

"But you're telling me I have an uncle out there? A living blood relative?"

"Yes."

"Then that means she kept me from my *family*. She lied and told me she was my aunt. She's had us on the run most of my life. There's no question that was all wrong!"

Okay, this was supposed to help her, and it was only riling her up even more. "Come on, Talia, give her a break. She had your safety and well-being in mind. People sometimes make bad choices out of fear. But don't doubt that she cares about you."

"If she cared about me, she would've told me the

truth, not kept it hidden away." She was back to pacing, this time an angry march from window to door and back again.

"Do you want to stop looking for her?"

She halted mid-step. "What?"

"Should we stop looking for her?"

"Of course not. She's still in danger. She's still… I'm just…" She shook her head and faced him. "No matter what she's done or how I feel, we still need to save her." A puzzled expression came over her face. "Why would you consider stopping the search?"

"I wasn't. I just want you to see that you do care about her. And despite what she did, she loves you. She's still your family too."

"She lied to me and hid the truth. That's not love. And that's not something family does."

"You might be the only family she really had."

"What are you talking about?"

"Did you ever stop to think about where she's from? Her family that she grew up with?"

She looked down and toed the wheel of the hospital bed. "No."

"Her family may have been connected to a Venezuelan drug cartel. Your uncle, Gregory, might be the only one who can help her at this point."

TWELVE

Talia pressed her fingertips to her temples, trying to work this new information into her brain as she walked back and forth in Noah's hospital room.

Sally wasn't her aunt. But she did have an uncle now. Her father's brother. Her immediate family was killed, but not in a car accident. They were murdered by some gang hired by an unknown enemy. And now someone kidnapped Sally, burned down their ranch, shot up her home, and—was it all some bizarre nightmare?

"Talia?" Noah's voice reached through her muddled thoughts. "Are you okay? We'll find, Sally. I promise."

She wasn't sure how she felt about Sally right now. So many feelings were ricocheting through her. On a good day she had a very tentative handle on slippery, ambiguous things like emotions. This was about the furthest thing from a good day.

But no matter how she felt, finding Sally was a must. If nothing else, Sally held too many secrets. Secrets Talia needed to hear.

She stepped up to Noah's bedside, arms folded across her chest.

"Why do you think my…uncle—" it sounded so foreign "—can help us find her?"

"He's rich. Connected."

"Rich?"

"Like mega-rich. He broadcast commercials on television stations across the country asking the public for help in finding you. I can't believe you haven't seen them."

"I never watch broadcast television, ironically, because I hate commercials. And I would rather read. Work and the ranch always keep me busy."

"I wasn't lying when I always wondered what happened to you." He searched her gaze, his brown eyes intense. He grabbed her hand. "The first time I saw your uncle's commercial seven months ago, it sparked hope. I remembered the stories Carol would tell us. And I thought maybe I could find you. Try to help find answers to what happened. Now I've found you. Sally wanted to wait, but your uncle would have resources, tech, people we can hire to help find her. The only thing I have are the memories, the stories that helped connect me to you and the Owyhees. But now? I think we should go to him."

It made sense. Besides, she had no home to go to. The ranch was a pile of rubble, and her cottage, though standing, had to be riddled with bullet holes. Not to mention there were still people trying to kill her.

Noah swung his legs over the side of the bed. "We should go to Gregory. He would have a vested interest in finding Sally and the people who took her. Justice for your family."

"Why do you think his wealth will make a difference? How is it going to help us find Sally?"

"Because we know more now. We are right on their

tail, not following a cold trail from over twenty years ago. It's time for you to step back into your life as Anna Coleson. The Coleson Company has state-of-the-art navigational technology. They probably have tools we've never dreamed of that could help."

Step into her life as Anna Coleson? How was she supposed to do that? She didn't know who Anna Coleson was. And everything about Talia Knowles was adding up to be a fabricated lie. But Noah was right. It was time to see her uncle and hopefully he could help them find Sally. And answers. She desperately needed some answers.

Uncle. Still so strange-sounding.

She looked out the west-facing window past the buildings, over the treetops scattered throughout the city, and toward the faint hills in the distance. She had family out there. Family that wanted her. Had been searching for her.

Family Sally kept her from. She had to have known about this uncle. And yet she never told Talia a thing.

A warm hand on her shoulder pulled her attention back to Noah. "Look, Talia, I know I should've told you earlier about Gregory, but I was trying to keep my word to Sally—"

He was sorry? She turned to face him. "You have no reason to apologize, Noah. You're the first person in my life to tell me the truth, to treat me with that kind of respect. To tell me things everyone else thought I was too weak or stupid to understand. Or maybe they considered me incapable of handling it." She squeezed his hand. "But you were different. You told me. Thank you."

Standing this close, she studied his eyes, such a delicious shade of brown, with dapples of gold reflecting the sunlight streaming in through the window. Funny how she couldn't even recall what color eyes Danny had. They had never captured her like this. And Noah's touch—what it did to her. It was more exhilarating than riding at a full gallop on the back of a strong horse, the wind whipping through her hair, the hint of risk and danger mingled with immense freedom that made her feel alive.

A nurse burst in and broke the spell. "Well, no wonder all the alarms were going off at the nurse station. What happened to your IV, young man?" She bustled around the bed, trying to stick sensors back on Noah's chest.

Noah sat there staring at Talia, oblivious to the nurse. "What do you say, Talia? Ready to go to California?"

Was she?

No matter what she was feeling, Uncle Gregory was their best option.

Talia looked at the nurse. "We need to leave now. Can you please get the doctor to order the discharge papers?"

"Leave?"

"Yes, we are leaving as soon as possible. I have a family reunion I'm late for."

The superstore parking lot bustled with people and overflowing shopping carts. Noah watched as a woman led a trail of children past his truck on the way to the store entrance. The line of kids giggled and held hands, the oldest helping herd the younger ones. But it was the toddler in the seat of the cart that everyone could hear. The little guy screamed. His mouth open wide, snot and tears running down his chubby face, he fought against the belt that strapped him in and kicked his legs until one of his shoes flew off. One of his siblings picked it up, and they continued on their merry (and not-so-merry) way, ignoring the tantrum the boy pitched.

While it felt better to get out of that hospital and behind the wheel of his old red Ford that Ed helped retrieve from Talia's cottage, part of him related all too well with the toddler.

He should feel better. Freer. He'd finally told Talia about Gregory. But he'd escaped one prison only to be trapped by another. It wasn't just the clunky medical boot and damaged lungs that he fought.

Talia had to inform him he was the first person to tell her the truth and make it out like he was some big hero.

He was no hero.

He groaned and dropped his head to the steering wheel. He promised Kelley he'd keep her safe. A white cross in the military cemetery now bore her name. He needed to get Talia to Gregory and leave her far behind, no matter what he felt about her.

Well, it's not like he was in love with her or anything. Right?

How could he be falling in love with a woman he'd met a few days ago? Reality check: she was a soon-to-be-rich heiress and he was a struggling rancher. And he couldn't keep the people he cared about safe. He was too much like his father to be suitable for any woman.

Thanks a lot, Dad. Yet again, the curse of being a Dillard wreaked havoc on his life.

Best to get her to San Jose as soon as possible, collect his money to save the ranch and get out of her life.

Talia opened the passenger door. "You got your prescriptions?"

"Yes, Dr. Talia. Do you have everything you need for a little road trip?"

"Yup." She still had one foot outside. "Are you sure it's okay to drive all the way to California? I could fly alone, and you'd be free to go live your life and—"

"Face it. You're not getting rid of me that easy. I told you I would help you find Sally, and that's what I'm going to do."

"Why don't we simply call my uncle, and we can see if he'll help us? It would be more efficient."

"There have been a lot of fake Anna Colesons that have popped up over the years. Gregory is very skeptical. Believe me, he will want to see you with his own two eyes. The sooner we get there, the sooner we can make our case for Sally."

She sighed, closed the door, and then became very still.

"Talia, don't you want to see him?"

He touched her sleeve, but she continued to stare out the window away from him until she turned and burst out, "What if he doesn't want me? What if I disappoint him?"

"How could he be disappointed in you?"

"Because I'm…me. I'm weird and hyper-focused on horses. Animals make more sense to me than people. I'm blunt and—"

He cupped her cheek and traced her freckles with his thumb. Wow, she was beautiful. It wasn't the beauty that the world liked to recognize on a magazine cover. But her depth. Her transparency. Like a precious gemstone, its rarity the exact thing that made it so valuable.

"Hey. He's going to love you. You are authentic and passionate and so smart. And I have to say, I don't know what Danny was thinking not seeing what an amazing gift he had, because you're also drop-dead gorgeous."

Her breath caught. "You...you think I'm pretty?" Her eyes sparked with curiosity. She wasn't fishing for a compliment or wanting platitudes. She really didn't know.

"You don't know how unique and beautiful you are, do you?"

She shook her head.

"Tell you what, we've got a long drive ahead of us. You just rest, enjoy the scenery, and before you know it, you'll be back with your family."

Her smile held hope. "Thank you, Noah Landers."

But once she realized who he really was, she wouldn't look at him like that anymore.

He was living a lie. He was no hero. Just ask Kelley Donalds's family.

THIRTEEN

Noah thought she was pretty? *Drop-dead gorgeous* were his exact words. The thought made her smile as she gazed out over the desolate Nevada landscape. Snow-capped hills and peaks in the distance, scrub brush and tumbleweeds dotting the swells that hugged the interstate. Idaho and the Owyhees behind them. California farther down the road in front of them. Country music from the radio serenading them as they rolled down the interstate.

How was it that this guy made her find hope again? Made her feel like she belonged.

She was so sure after calling off her wedding that she'd remain single for the rest of her life. But if a guy like Noah saw something in her, maybe there was still hope for a family of her own someday. Someone like Noah to share a life with. Raise children with. Build a legacy with.

And to know she had an uncle? It changed everything. She wasn't as alone as she thought.

The light shifted as a pile of clouds blew in and blocked the sun. Just when she was starting to warm up and enjoy the sunshine. And like the shadows outside the truck, thoughts of Sally invaded, dimming the warmth and light.

She still didn't know what to do with Sally. Thinking

about her made her whole body go tense. If she were a horse, she would stomp and kick.

Noah glanced at her. "What's going on with you over there? You look mad."

Anger. That's what it was. "I *am* mad."

"Why?"

"Because Sally lied to me."

"Yeah, but she lied about who she was to protect you. Can't you see that?"

"Maybe when I was a preschooler and she had to secure new identities, Sally had to make up this whole charade about being my aunt. But at some point, she should've let me in on the story. Instead, I'm the last to know. Again." Talia's eyes smarted. She turned away from Noah and watched the blurry fence posts along the highway. "She was the one person I trusted."

Broken trust. What was she supposed to do with that?

Noah sighed. "Yeah, families are complicated."

"She's not even family though! *And* she let me believe I had no other family in the world. But that whole time, she was the one that kept me from my uncle."

"She also saved your life. Running with you, giving you a new identity, might be why you're alive today. I wasn't there over the years, but I know your safety and care have always been Sally's priorities."

"She lied. How can you defend her?"

"I'm not defending the lies, Talia. I'm trying to get you to see her heart. That woman loves you like a daughter. She took care of you. She'd die for you. That's family."

"Yeah, well, there's never a good reason to lie." She turned back to the window, whispering more to her reflection than to her companion. "She should've told me the truth."

"What will you do when we find her?"

What would she do? Logic said she wasn't trustworthy. Therefore, Talia should cut her out of her life and move on.

But a big gaping hole opened inside when she thought of her life without Sally being a part of it. "I don't know," she finally said.

"Do you think you could ever—I don't know—forgive her?"

"I spent my whole life thinking I'm one person only to learn I'm someone else. Anna Coleson. I've been separated from my only family because of her. How am I supposed to pretend that didn't happen?"

"I don't think that's what forgiveness means." Noah reached over and turned off the radio. "Talia, sometimes people can love you and still do the wrong thing. *Especially* in families. To forgive them doesn't mean we pretend what they did was right. It means we choose to let go of bitterness and our right to get payback. It's never about pretending it didn't happen or saying what they did was okay."

But the injustice of it all burned inside. Wrong was still wrong. Nothing changed that. She looked down at her stuffed horse, Sunny, in her hands, twirling one of the braids around her finger. The only stuffed animal from her childhood that escaped the fire because it was in the back seat of the car they borrowed.

Sally kept the truth about having an uncle from her for decades. All this time, as Talia pined for family, for connections, to be a normal kid, Sally knew he was out there. Yet she kept this fact hidden.

She couldn't get past that. "She doesn't deserve to be forgiven."

"Forgiveness can't be earned or it's not really for-giveness."

"What do you mean?"

"Forgiveness isn't like someone paying back a debt that they owed you and now you're even. That's resti-tution. It's different. Forgiveness is canceling the debt even though the other person hasn't paid back a cent."

"How am I supposed to do that?"

"You can bring your hurt, bring that offense, to God. No one understands your pain more than Him. But then you leave it in His hands instead of needing to get even. It will allow you to heal."

"Is that what you do?"

"I try. And when I look back on all I've been forgiven for…well, it's pretty hard to hold a grudge against any-one else."

"But how can I ever trust her again?"

"That's a different story. Trust *is* something that should be earned and will have to be rebuilt. That will take some time. But you can forgive her right now."

Talia mulled it over, repeating his words in her head. *No one understands your pain more than Him.*

But how did she leave it with God? How did she move on?

Noah nudged her arm. "It doesn't make what she did right, but at the end of the day, I hope you do see that Sally loves you. You would be missing out on that love if you hold on to the hurt and cut her out of your life."

Her shoulders sagged as she laid her head back on the headrest. It kind of made sense.

But she still wasn't sure she was capable of doing any of it. Forgiving or trusting the woman who raised her. She had never been so alone.

* * *

Noah concentrated on the road instead of the pain meds and antibiotics bumping around in his stomach or the floral scent wafting from Talia. The landscape hadn't changed much in the last two hundred miles. Still a lot of road in the middle of a lot of scrubby desert and very few cities or signs of civilization.

His thighs grew numb. He rolled his shoulders and tried to ease the kink in his neck. His body didn't bother him nearly as much as his heart did.

He knew it. He was falling for Talia. But he didn't deserve her. He liked her passion, her transparency. She didn't play games. She was pure and true to herself. But she was in danger the longer she was with him. And the longer she was with him, the more he wanted to be her hero. But Gregory had a lot more to offer her. He would be able to keep her safe.

So every mile brought them closer to her uncle and a forever goodbye.

A heavy weight settled on his soul.

The truck engine rattled.

Talia stopped tapping her fingers on her leg. "What was that?"

He checked the gas gauge. "The ol' girl is telling me she needs some fuel. Nothing to worry about."

Another clacking sounded from under the hood.

"You sure about that?"

Noah tried to infuse confidence in his words. "She's fine. But probably wouldn't hurt to add some more oil too. We're coming up on an exit with a big travel center. I'll check her there."

"Good. I need a restroom."

Ten minutes later, Noah pulled into the travel center

and up to the pump. Talia grabbed the small duffel bag with the few things she brought with her and rushed into the casino/convenience store/truck stop as he lifted the hood. The smell of gasoline and burning oil made him cough, too redolent of the smoke he inhaled in the fire last night.

And of course, that would be when his phone rang. Justin. He waited for the coughing spell to pass before he answered. "Hey, Justin. Were you able to find anything?"

"Man, you sure have a knack for landing in a tough spot. This Vasquez cartel is serious business."

"What do you mean?"

"Talked to a buddy at the DEA. The Vasquezes supply a lot of cocaine to our US streets. They are ruthless too. Violent. You don't want to get on their bad side. For the most part they stay in Venezuela, and the DEA isn't sure how the drugs get into the US yet. I mentioned the East Fourteenth Street gang, and they'll look into it, see if there's any connection."

"Do you think Carol's family is connected with the Vasquez cartel? You got a picture of that photo I sent you?"

"Yeah. But the original would be better. Can you send it?"

"It burned in the fire. Thankfully I took a picture of it and sent it to you before the house burned down."

"Right. We've got some people working on it. The one guy is definitely Sebastian Vasquez forty years ago."

Noah coughed again until his throat was raw. When the spasm passed, he took a long, careful breath.

"You doing alright? You sound horrible."

Noah limped over to the pump and opened the gas tank. "Just some smoke inhalation and a broken foot."

"Oh yeah. The fire. Talked to the fire marshal there, too. You'll never guess what started it."

"What?"

"Bombs, probably dropped by drones."

Noah fumbled with the gas tank cap. It fell to the ground and rolled under the truck. "You're kidding."

"Nope. Two bombs dropped on the house. One hit that shed attached to the barn. Probably missed its mark, which was good for you, gave you time to save those animals."

Maybe, but the panicked look in Zeus's eyes might haunt him for a while. Noah bent down and used his crutch to reach the cap.

"This is serious. You better be careful. You sure you don't want help protecting her?"

"I'm taking her to Gregory Coleson. I'm sure he'll have security and a protection detail for her. Do you think it might be this Vasquez cartel after her?"

"After what I read about them, I sure hope not. We just reopened Anna's case. It's going to take a while, but we've got people looking for the nanny and we're doing our best."

"Thanks, Justin. Hey, are you doing okay? You know, since coming home, transitioning stateside?"

A short pause spoke volumes.

"Yeah. I'm good. I mean, it's not everything I thought it would be, but it's…fine. Enough about me. Just wanted to let you know what I found so far."

"Appreciate it."

"Semper fi, brother. I'm here in San Jose, flew in this

morning to help this team since I had the inside scoop thanks to you. Stop in and see me when you get here."

"Okay. I'll be there in Cali by tonight. Just gassing up here in The-Middle-of-Nowhere, Nevada, but we're only a couple hours from the border."

"Be careful, Noah. Whatever you're mixed up in with this woman is huge. Someone wants her dead."

Noah ended the call. When this was all said and done, he should visit Justin in Montana and see how he was handling everything, especially since being dumped by his fiancée. Their friend Cade said it was pretty ugly.

Until then, he had plenty to do. Noah hobbled back to the hood and took a look. He might've downplayed the soundness of his truck. She was running rough, but she should get them to San Jose at least. After saving the Landers Ranch, maybe Noah would have to buy something newer.

He ran a hand down the faded red body.

He didn't want something newer. Grandpa Landers's truck wasn't something easy to replace.

He wiped the dipstick and dipped it again to check the oil level.

But wants didn't always matter in life. If someone couldn't do the job, they weren't the right person, no matter how much they wanted it. If the truck was damaged beyond repair, he'd have to get a different one.

So, yeah, maybe he wanted to be Talia's hero, but he failed to do that for Kelley. He wasn't right for the job. Damaged beyond repair might be an apt description for him too.

He sighed and looked back to the interstate, cars and commercial trucks zooming past. They would be traveling close to his own ranch in Robin Valley. It would be

nice to stop and see his mom, make sure she was holding up okay. But Talia's safety came first.

He replaced the dipstick. "Hold out, girl. We gotta
get her to her uncle."

After scrubbing her hands in the surprisingly clean
restroom and changing the shirt she spilled ketchup on,
Talia bypassed the dark cave-like casino and wandered
through the aisles of the convenience store. She must
be hungry again. The smell of hot dogs and microwave
burritos made her mouth water. There wasn't a healthy
food option in the place, but at this point it didn't matter. She paid for a gas station corn dog and took a bite
while waiting for the change.

A look out the window showed Noah on the phone,
just starting to pump gas. She wasn't ready to sit in the
chilly cab again. She munched on her treat and watched
the television in the corner behind the cashier.

A name on the screen caught her attention. The corn
dog froze halfway to her mouth. The few bites she'd already eaten turned to ice in her stomach.

"Help Me Find Anna Coleson" ran as a banner under
an older distinguished-looking man, maybe young fif-
ties. His light brown hair was peppered with gray but
cut stylishly and in such a way that drew attention to his
firm jawline and piercing blue eyes.

Talia dropped her corn dog and lunged for the cashier.
"Turn that up, please!" She pointed to the TV.

The cashier looked at the screen and shook her head.
"That commercial? We've all seen it a thousand times."

"Please!"

Maybe her desperation came through, and the gray-haired woman took pity. Whatever the reason, she rolled her eyes and turned up the volume.

The man pleaded. "—so I'm asking you today to help me find my niece. Anna Coleson. Please call the number below if you have any information. I'm offering a reward for any tips leading to her discovery." A picture of her as a child side-by-side with some computer-generated photo that was meant to look like her filled the screen. The hair was way too light, the eyes too far apart and the lips kinda thin. Maybe with a lot of makeup or hair styling she'd look like that. But it was close enough. It was supposed to be her.

"Honey, you okay?" The cashier leaned over the counter. "You're not going to get sick on my floor, are you? I just mopped."

"Uh, no." Though vomiting seemed very possible at the moment. It was true. She had an uncle, and he had been searching for her. She studied his face. His voice that broke as he looked into the camera, begging for help. She really was wanted. She had a family. A family Sally had kept her from.

"Child, you okay? You've got some color coming back, but you went pretty pale." Her hand stilled. "In fact…you look kind of like that…" She turned back to the TV, but a game show was already playing. She shook her head and chuckled. "I've watched that silly thing so many times, I'm starting to think I see that girl everywhere."

Without a word or smile, Talia turned and walked back to the hallway with the restrooms. A taste of seeing her own flesh-and-blood relative and she wanted more.

Along with a sign for showers, there was another pointing to the internet/computer station. She plopped her bag down on the floor and sat at one of the computers. She quickly typed "Anna Coleson" in the search bar.

A list with millions of hits popped up, including social media profiles for the many Anna Colesons in the world. No, she needed something more specific. She typed "Coleson family explosion San Jose California."

She read the top article listed, quickly scanning the words, devouring them and yet wanting to spit them back out as soon as she made sense of them. Explosion. Six deaths. No body found for Anna Coleson or nanny Carol Force. Henry Dillard, bodyguard suspect in helping gang execute the bombing.

Henry Dillard. The name jiggled something loose in her memory.

Dillard.

Noah Dillard.

She could hear a voice calling, *Noah Dillard, you get down from there right this minute.*

Her sister Ava said that. And Talia mimicked it after that, the bossy tone and everything. She loved the way it rolled off her tongue. "Noah Dillard, stop this minute. Noah Dillard, give me a horsey ride. Noah Dillard, put me down."

The memory was so clear.

Tears pricked her eyes. Maybe her past wasn't all lost. But why did Noah go by Landers now? What made him change his name? As she skimmed an article about her uncle and his recent campaign to find her, she gasped at the reward amount he was offering.

Noah said Gregory was rich, but a million-dollar reward?

Was that why Noah was so adamant about bringing her to Gregory himself? Here she thought he was simply a nice guy, but a million dollars was a huge incentive. He said he wanted to find her, but he never mentioned the money.

Talia clicked on another article.

A beefy hand smelling of gasoline and onions slapped against her mouth, cutting off a scream. "I've lost a lot of time looking for you," a voice whispered in her ear. "If you want to live, you'll stand up slowly and follow my directions. And don't try to resist or I'll kill your boyfriend too."

If her body hadn't frozen completely, maybe she would have fought back or tried to follow the man's command. But she lost all muscle control.

When she didn't move, the hand wrapped around her neck and pulled her up. A heavy arm dropped on her shoulder, trapping her close to the onion odor and the gun he held jabbed into her side.

She should scream. Fight. Something. But her body wouldn't obey. Panic seized her voice. Her breath stuck in her lungs as he dragged her out a back entrance and stuffed her into the trunk of a car, shutting her into darkness.

Noah searched the aisles of the convenience store again. Nothing. Talia was too practical to gamble for money, but maybe she wandered into the casino. It didn't seem like her, but where else could she be?

A thorough sweep around the slot machines revealed nothing but an oncoming headache thanks to the heavy perfume one lady wore that didn't quite cover up the smell of stale cigarette smoke.

Come on. She had to be here somewhere. A frisson of panic raced through him. This was taking too long.

The only other place would be the women's restroom or the showers. Noah hobbled on his crutches toward the bathrooms again. He peeked into the computer station. No Talia.

But a headline in bold letters on the computer screen glared back at him. "Coleson Tragedy Rocks San Jose."

Noah fell into the plastic chair at the computer. A search on Anna Coleson. She had been here. And not long ago, according to the time stamp listed.

A small duffel on the floor caught his eye. That was Talia's. He opened it up. One of those clear makeup bags with toiletries, clothes, and her stuffed animal. Sunny.

No way she would've left this behind willingly.

She was in trouble.

Noah slung the long strap of the bag across his body and moved to the hallway. How had these people found her so quickly? He'd let her down again, and she was in danger. Frustration and fear for her boiled over. He forced himself to take a calm breath and think.

He looked both ways in the hall. If someone took Talia, they wouldn't go through the main store. They would've used a more discreet exit. He moved toward the back of the building, pulling the gun Ed had pressed into his hands before he left out of its holster.

Around the corner was an employee break room, the back door cracked open with a rock. He rushed as fast as he could on crutches and shoved the door open, just in time to see a big sedan pull away. Two men in the front, and no one else that he could see. But she had to be in that car. They headed toward the vast desert. There was no other sign of life this far back in the parking lot with darkness closing in.

He couldn't let them get away.

He lifted his gun as the car turned to the right. He didn't earn a marksman badge for nothing. Aiming carefully at the front wheel, he squeezed the trigger. The first shot missed, but the second shot blew out the tire. He couldn't risk hurting Talia, but that would slow them down.

Sure enough, the car swerved and then stopped. A tall Asian man came out the passenger side, shooting. Not knowing where Talia was in the vehicle, Noah didn't return fire, but instead dove for cover behind the metal trash container just outside the break room door.

If he could lure the two men away from the car, he wouldn't hesitate to shoot back. Noah waited, listening for heavy footfalls and praying the bullets flying his way would miss their mark and not ricochet.

Footsteps didn't come. Instead, sounds of the trunk opening and Talia's cry stopped his heart.

"You want this girl to live? If you do, you better come out here right now!"

Noah came around the corner of the container slowly. He laid his gun on the asphalt and stood again on his good leg and showed his empty hands. "Don't hurt her!"

The man he saw from the passenger side held Talia by her hair. She was still kneeling in the trunk. But he yanked her arm and dragged her out of the car.

Noah hopped closer with his crutches until the man yelled, "Stop right there."

The driver stood outside his door and scanned the parking lot. "We gotta get out of here. Come on, before someone calls the cops."

"Then go find us another ride," his partner yelled. The driver rushed around the corner of the building and disappeared.

While his head was turned away from him, Noah clenched his jaw against the pain and moved two more steps closer to Talia, his gaze never leaving the gun held to her head.

He made eye contact with her. "Are you okay?"

She sent him a shaky nod.

"Stop moving!" The big guy swung his arm and aimed the gun at Noah's chest.

"I just want the girl. Your partner is right. Cops are probably on their way." Infusing as much calm as he could muster into his voice, he moved a little closer. And as long as the gun was aimed at him, Talia would have a chance. "You should just leave her and run for it. She'll only slow you down. And we won't press charges."

"Like I'm scared of you pressing charges. If I don't come back with her, I don't come back at all. Now stop moving!"

The man's hand shook. He was scared alright. But not of Noah. He feared failing whoever he worked for. Desperation made him unpredictable. But three more steps and Noah would be within striking distance. Everything inside him coiled, ready to snag Talia out of her captor's grip and protect her. He might be injured, but he could use his crutch as a weapon, and he would do whatever it took to keep her safe.

But the man backed up, dragging Talia with him. "Move any closer and you're a dead man."

FOURTEEN

Talia's breath hitched. Her head tilted back at an awkward angle with her hair snagged firmly in the stranger's hand. She almost lost her balance as he yanked her back a few more steps. She couldn't catch her breath. Every muscle shivered as she took in the scene.

There was a gun pointed at Noah's chest, and she was in the grasp of a very dangerous man.

She didn't know a lot about reading facial expressions, but she knew down to her core that Noah would battle for her. Or maybe he was fighting for the million dollars she'd just read about in the online article. Either way, the stubborn soldier was not going down without a fight.

And somehow it brought everything else into focus and filled her with a sense of purpose. She couldn't let Noah go down protecting her.

He had already lost too much. He was shot, trampled on and injured. She wouldn't be responsible for more.

Steadying her breath, she forced her mind to remember all the self-defense techniques Sally had her learn. But how could she risk a shot fired in Noah's direction?

The man's arm was too long for her to reach the gun. If it wasn't pointing at Noah, she could make a move.

A creak from the break room door broke the silence and drew their attention back to the building.

"Get out of here!" The gun barrel pointed at the unsuspecting employee who had probably wandered out for his smoke break.

And it was just the distraction Talia needed. She slammed her fist back with a well-positioned punch to the groin and ground the heel of her boot into the man's foot. He loosened his hold on her, enough for her to break away as he howled in pain. At the same time, Noah sprang, knocking the gun out of the man's hand with his crutch.

Talia ran after the gun while Noah blocked a punch and delivered an uppercut to man's jaw. The big man's head snapped back. He staggered and fell to the ground.

"Run!" Noah pointed. He hopped on his good foot and used his crutch to move to the trash container, where he picked up his own gun and her duffel bag off the ground. The man lying on the asphalt behind them didn't move. "We've gotta find a way out of here."

Talia jogged as Noah limped and hopped along the side of the building toward the front. She leaned against the cold stucco wall and tried to catch her breath, her body buzzing with adrenaline. "Think we can make it to your truck?"

"Maybe. But I don't think my truck can outrun these guys if they find a car. We need to outsmart them." Noah stopped before they reached the corner of the front of the building.

Talia pushed herself off the wall and looked around. This truck stop was in the middle of the desert. There wasn't a town to hide in. No other buildings in sight. Just the interstate running on the other side of the parking lot. Cars and semis rushing past. "We can't stay here."

And Noah, injured as he was, wouldn't get far on foot.

"Maybe we can hitch a ride." He pointed toward the rows of diesel fuel pumps and semitrucks lined up at them.

"But we need to get to California." Now that Talia had watched the commercial herself, her own uncle pleading for her, she needed to see him. The sooner she did, the sooner she could be out of Noah's life and all the injury and harm she'd already caused him. And the sooner she would be with family. Closer to answers. Hopefully Gregory would be able to fill in the blanks of the last twenty-five years.

But the thought of never seeing Noah again wasn't a pleasant one. In fact, it muddled up everything she felt inside even more.

"We better go. Looks like our bad guy found himself a car." Noah pointed to where a gray SUV took a sharp turn into the parking lot and the driver that originally grabbed Talia earlier waved them down and jumped in.

Great. The bad guys had backup, and now she and Noah were outnumbered. They'd soon find the other man Noah knocked out behind the building.

As the SUV sped around the other side of the travel center, Noah nudged her forward. "Come on. We've got to get out of here."

They crossed in front of the main entrance over to the diesel pumps and lines of semitrucks.

"Noah, where are we going?" She couldn't say why she felt the need to whisper, but she did. Noah hobbled with confidence, like he had a plan. Like he belonged.

She was following him blindly along, as clueless as ever. There weren't many places to hide, and that SUV would be back around any second.

He stopped and nodded to the truck at the first pump. "There!"

"What about it?" The logo of a hammer and nails with a robin on the side didn't seem very promising.

"My hometown has a hardware and feed store. They get deliveries from this company. There aren't very many branches of that store. I'm guessing the driver is heading there now for the Saturday morning delivery."

"It's going to San Jose?"

"No. It's going to Robin Valley. My family's ranch is there. If we can get that far, I'll have someone pick us up, and I can get us another vehicle. We'll only be three or four hours from San Jose."

It sounded like the best option. "Better hurry. Looks like the driver is ready to leave."

Noah approached the lanky man climbing into the driver's seat. "Excuse me, any chance you're going to Robin Valley?"

The driver nodded. "Yup. With a stop in Reno."

"Then you're an answer to my prayers." Noah pulled out that charming grin. No hint that they were in danger or that any moment bullets could be flying their way. He continued his story as if it were a normal Friday afternoon. "My truck broke down, and we really need to get to my ranch as soon as possible. If we could hitch a ride to Robin Valley—since you're heading there anyway—we'd be super grateful."

The stranger looked over at Talia and back at Noah. "I don't—"

A squeal of tires in the parking lot and yelling from

behind the building stopped the man's words. Those guys must be close.

"I've got cash for your troubles too." Noah pulled out a couple of fifty-dollar bills from his wallet and had the man's attention once more. "And I'll double that when we get there."

The money must've made a difference since the driver suddenly had a wide smile on his face and shook Noah's hand. "Alrighty then. Hop in and we'll be on our way."

Could they really trust this guy? Noah urged her forward and probably saw the question in her eyes, because he leaned in and whispered in her ear. "We'll be alright. Just a few more hours to Reno, and if he's shady at all, we'll cut ties there and find a different way home. But we have to leave *now*."

Talia looked behind her. She couldn't see anything, but those men would be here any second. Her options were narrowed down to this.

She stuffed aside her reservations and climbed in the cab of the truck, where she soon found herself situated between Noah and a little brown-and-white Chihuahua.

As they pulled back out onto the interstate and drove away, the tightening in Talia's chest eased. Each mile took them farther away from the men who wanted her dead, and closer to her uncle.

With the warmth of the cab and the safety of Noah's presence, Talia leaned her head back on the seat and closed her eyes. The rush from the adrenaline drained away, leaving a heavy weariness. She had no energy for friendly discussion with the chatty driver. She would have to leave that for Noah. She settled further into the seat, and within seconds she fell asleep on his shoulder.

* * *

Noah looked down at the woman asleep at his side, leaning into him. Her head lay on his shoulder. Though he lost all feeling in his left arm, he didn't dare move or disturb her. It was the first time since she rushed into the Jordan Creek Ranch barn that he saw her at peace.

He longed to brush back the wavy caramel-colored lock of hair that fell over her eye. Or to feel the soft creaminess of her cheek.

Noah wanted nothing more than to do so, but it would be foolish to start something that would only lead to more heartbreak. What did he have to offer her? She would soon be protected and well provided for once they reached Gregory.

Still, he didn't mind when her head slid from his shoulder and nuzzled into his chest and she released a soft sigh. He would tuck away this sweet memory and try really hard to remember his mission. Keep Talia safe and get her to her uncle in San Jose.

Although maybe an hour or two at Landers Ranch would be a good thing. She'd always loved it there as a little girl. The only time she ever cried was when they had to leave. She hated leaving the horses. That's what gave Xander the idea to buy her a stuffed horse for her birthday that year. A horse she didn't have to say good-bye to. The horse she still held in her hands as she slept.

The driver, Barney, hummed along with the old-time country station on the radio. "Looks like we're getting close to Robin Valley. Wish I could take y'all the way to San Jose, but this is my last stop. I leave the truck at the loading dock, and stay at a hotel here. I can drop you off at your place."

"This is great. I can't thank you enough, Barney."

Talia roused as they rolled into Noah's hometown of Robin Valley. He was surprised at the nostalgia and relief hitting him. He'd been gone for overseas tours multiple times, years with each stint. This time he'd been gone only seven months and wasn't even that far away. But somehow seeing the familiar white steeple of Robin Valley Community Church, the old-fashioned-looking streetlights lining Main Street, and the farm supply store where he had his first job, and all the comfortable sights of a small town asleep under the stars, brought a peace he didn't know he'd been missing.

Yes, it was the right decision to bring Talia home.

Barney turned down Clover Road, weaving through the foothills.

"That's our place. The next driveway. If you take the next left turn, you can loop back to town."

Barney stopped at the end of the driveway, by the rusty mailbox. Noah dug through his wallet for more cash and offered it to him. After waving goodbye, he and Talia passed under the log Landers Ranch sign hanging over the entrance to their property. Noah was home.

They moved toward the log house with the wide front porch lit with warm yellow lights shining from the windows, beckoning them. A hint of campfire smoke and Mom's famous chili wafted on the breeze. "If my nose is right, we came at the perfect time to enjoy some chili and cinnamon rolls." Noah's stomach grumbled.

Talia looked unsure. "I'm not crazy about spicy food. But I am hungry."

"Don't worry. Mom always makes the chili mild. I spice mine up with hot sauce and red pepper flakes. Add a little sour cream and cheese and you're in heaven."

She didn't look convinced, but before he could open

his mouth to defend his mother's chili further, the woman herself came out onto the porch. "Noah, that you? What in the world are you doing here? And why are you on crutches?"

She rushed toward him and engulfed him in a hug. She still hadn't gained all the weight back, but there was nothing better than having those bony arms wrapped around him, squeezing tight.

"Sorry, Mom, for dropping in without any notice. We ran into a little trouble and needed a place to stay. And we'll need a vehicle too."

"Obviously you have a lot of explaining to do before we address any of that. Why don't you come on inside, and you can tell me what's going on." She turned to Talia. "Who did you bring—" Her hands flew to her mouth, and her eyes shimmered with tears. "Oh my. Anna Coleson. It's really you!"

Talia looked at him, uncertainty written all over her face.

"Tal, this is my mom, Marcy."

"Nice to meet you, ma'am." Talia stuck out a stiff hand.

Mom ignored it and hugged her too. "Anna, I can't believe it's really you."

"Mom, she goes by Talia now."

"Actually, I've been thinking of going back to Anna Coleson, so call me either. It's fine."

That was news. And was it just him, or was Talia acting a little weird? Well, weird for Talia. She didn't act like other women he knew, and he liked that about her. But something about the wariness in her eyes concerned him.

"Well, come on in out of the cold and have some chili.

Good thing I made extra tonight." Mom ushered Talia into the house, and Noah hobbled behind on the crutches.

Yeah, it was good to be home.

And, okay, maybe delaying the family reunion with her uncle was a little selfish, but it was good for Talia too. Mom was the perfect person to help Talia relax with everything weighing on her mind.

As much as he was looking forward to showing Gregory he could be trusted to find his niece and keep her safe, and in that small way return some honor to his family, it would be the end of this connection with Talia.

And that, he wasn't ready for.

Leaving behind the chilled night and walking into the Landers ranch home, Talia was caught in such a swirl of emotions she couldn't begin to untangle them. But one sniff of the sweet cinnamon in the air and her mouth watered. Hunger. That was one sensation identified. If she could just ignore the rest, she'd be great.

As they walked through the living room, Talia noticed the deep navy-and-scarlet-patterned rug, a rustic-looking coffee table, and a bowl full of spheres, balls of twine and twigs resting on the ledge of a stone hearth. It was just like Noah had described back in her cottage.

And those touches added something to the room. They made it feel like more than a place to stay. They added color and warmth. They made the space feel… loved.

Before she could ponder any of that, Noah's mother led them to the kitchen. Sure enough, a fruity-smelling candle glowed on the kitchen counter.

Marcy pulled out a chair at the long farmhouse table.

"Come on in and get settled here. I'll warm up some chili and put a pot of coffee on. Unless you prefer tea?"

"Coffee is great, Mrs. Landers." Talia sat at long dining room table.

The woman froze and shot a pointed look at Noah. She set a huge cinnamon roll in front of Talia and laid a hand on her shoulder. "Please call me Marcy. Mrs. Landers is my mother. I'm Marcy Dillard."

"Dillard?"

That's right. Noah Dillard. Talia turned to the man leaning on crutches in the doorway. "But why did you introduce yourself as Noah Landers? And it said Landers Ranch on the sign."

Marcy stirred a big pot on the stove top. "Landers is my maiden name. This ranch was settled by my grandfather, and we've always kept his name for the property and business. As far as Noah changing his name from Dillard to Landers is concerned—" she turned to him "—care to explain, son?"

He was shrugging out of his jacket and mumbled, "Not really." He looked at Talia. "Just call her Marcy. We're not big on formality around here." He snagged his crutches and left the room.

So that's how it was going to be. He wanted to hear all about her past but didn't trust her with *his*. And there was still the question of this reward. Did he really care about her, or did he just want the money?

Marcy watched him leave with a sigh. "Don't mind him, Anna. He's not usually so surly, but you stumbled on a touchy subject. Now, how do you take your coffee?" She opened a cupboard, grabbing a mug from the middle shelf. The bottom shelf was chock full of medicines and supplements. Something for the pounding in her head would be nice.

"Do you have any ibuprofen in all those meds?"

"I'm sure I do." She dug until she found the right container. "How many?"

"Two for me. Noah should be taking some too. For his foot."

She shook pills into her hand. "When did that happen? He's usually good about keeping in touch with me and telling me what's going on."

"It only happened last night. He was trying to save my animals."

Marcy spun around. "Save your animals? From what?"

The fire.

That's right. A guy who was only helping her for the money wouldn't go to those extremes, would he? Protecting her to get the reward was one thing. But he put his own life in danger to help her animals. What did that mean?

Why were people so confusing?

"Anna?"

Right. Marcy still waited for an answer. "He saved my animals from the burning barn. Someone set it on fire. A horse stepped on Noah's foot. He has fractures on two of the metatarsals and proximal phalanges and over thirty stitches."

"Oh dear." Marcy looked back to the direction Noah left, worry so evident on her face even Talia could identify it. "I'll have to talk with him later. Here's your ibuprofen." Marcy went back to the cabinet and began setting out more bottles. "I should probably take my own meds before I forget to with all this excitement of you both showing up."

The medical side of her was curious. "What are you taking?" Talia asked.

"Oh, I'm just taking a few vitamins and other things. I tend to not absorb all the nutrients like I used to before the cancer treatments."

"Cancer?"

"Yes, but praise God I'm in remission now. Three years." She swallowed a handful of pills with one gulp of water.

"That had to be rough though."

Tears welled up in Marcy's eyes. "Yes. But it's amazing to see the evidence of God's goodness, even in the valley."

"Goodness? From cancer?"

Marcy sat next to Talia at the wooden table. Years of use showed in the scratches and dings on the surface, and years of love in the polished edges and shine. She traced one of the scratches with her fingertip. "Believe me, there's nothing good about cancer itself. Horrible disease. But even while fighting that sickness, God's mercies are evident."

"Like what?"

That might've sounded a little harsh. But it was hard to see any mercy at the moment. Talia had lost her family, her home. And, of course, the people closest to her betrayed and lied to her. Anybody who could find some mercy amid this must be a saint.

"Well, for one, it brought my Noah home."

"From the marines?"

Marcy nodded. "That boy has been through so much. As have you, Anna. And don't get me wrong. I'm proud of him. He made a fine soldier. But he's always had this drive to prove himself. I always wondered if joining the marines was more about that than a burning desire to serve in the military. Especially when he was so good with the horses."

"So he quit when you got cancer?"

"He didn't re-up as he had planned. Instead, he came home to take care of me, and the ranch. His sister, Janey, was going through a very difficult pregnancy at the time. She and her husband, Thomas, live down the road and help us on the ranch but had their hands full. Having Noah here to help me was a godsend."

"That must've made you happy."

"No mother likes to see her child give up their dreams, but I don't think the military was ever Noah's true passion. So, in that sense, yes, I was happy to have him back home." She sighed. "I just wish it hadn't come with such a burden."

"Burden? It's a beautiful ranch, and his family is here. Where's the burden in that?"

Marcy's shoulders sagged. "The burden of a struggling ranch and a mother with cancer is not an easy one to carry." She stood and went to stir the pot of chili again. "But we'll make it. Like you said, family is here. Together, we'll face whatever comes next." She scooped up a hearty serving and brought it to Talia. "Now, dear, enough about me and my woes. Tell me all about you. I can't believe you're here again after all these years."

Talia sprinkled shredded cheddar cheese and added a spoonful of sour cream to her chili. "Here again? I've been here before?"

"Oh yes. Our families would come up here to my dad's ranch a couple times a year to get out of the city and enjoy the fresh air. And sometimes Carol would make a special trip just with you because you loved the horses so much. Are you still crazy about them?"

Something about Marcy's warm hazel eyes drew a smile from her. Maybe she was remembering, and it was enough to let the guard inside slip a tiny bit. "I still love horses, yes. I'm a vet now. Equestrian care is my specialty. I have my own practice, and I volunteer for the state to work with the wild horses in Idaho."

Marcy laughed. "You and Noah. I swear it's like you have horses in your blood. At least, that's what your mom and I always said. Now, your brother, Xander, that boy was the one who wanted to be a soldier. He would follow Henry around, ask him all about security and hand-to-hand combat, while your sisters and Janey would put on fashion shows and write your own fashion magazines. I think I still have some up in the attic, in fact."

Talia forgot all about the chili and drank in the information about her family. Would it be inappropriate to beg for more?

Before she could, Noah came into the kitchen.

"Save any of that chili for me?"

Noah, the boy who loved horses, but became a soldier. The man who came home to take care of a sick mother and the family ranch. Her heart softened toward him, especially when he kissed his mother's cheek and reached for the painkillers she offered him. He didn't seem like the kind of guy who was doing all this for a reward.

Then Talia's back stiffened. Even so, she had no business feeling this way when so much of her life was unknown. She didn't even know what name to go by. Noah said she needed to step into her life as Anna Coleson, but she didn't know what that entailed. And her life as Talia Knowles was left behind in tatters, but there was still so much she needed to salvage. Not to mention it was hard enough for her to navigate basic relationships. How could she even entertain the idea of a possible romance?

Noah had a family, had his ranch. He didn't need her messing up his life any more than she already had.

Noah sipped his black coffee and stared out the bay window of the dining room. His foot was screaming, his shoulder throbbing. Not sure three ibuprofen would cut it. But downing them with a couple bowlfuls of Mom's chili and a cinnamon roll helped considerably.

Not that it would take away the pain of saying goodbye to Talia tomorrow. At this point they would wait until morning to set out in one of the ranch trucks. Talia looked pretty tired and didn't mind the delay. Hopefully she was sleeping again and getting the rest she needed.

Mom came and sat next to him at the table. "So, you found her. You accomplished what you set out to do."

He ran a finger through the icing left on the plate and licked it. "Yeah, and let me tell ya, it's been a wild ride ever since."

"Sounds like a lot happened since you called me three days ago to tell me you found Carol."

"You could say that."

"Where is Carol?"

"It's a long story."

"We have all night. And I'd like to know how my son ended up rescuing animals from a burning barn and breaking bones in his foot."

If only that was the worst of it. "I'll tell you, but you have to promise me you won't freak out."

"Noah Matthew." She leaned forward. "Spill it."

He tried to downplay the danger as much as possible while telling her what happened. He couldn't hide the crutches and ugly boot on his foot, but he left out the whole getting shot part, including Talia doing emergency surgery on his shoulder in an animal hospital. Some things a mom didn't need to know.

"Oh, Noah. Thank God you and Anna are okay. But what about Carol? She's gone, and someone is still after Anna?"

"That's why I'm trying to get Talia to Gregory. He'll have the resources to keep Talia safe and help find Sally. And remember my buddy, Justin? He's with the FBI now. He helped open up the Coleson case again."

Mom stared down at her left hand as she twirled the wedding ring she still wore. This had to be hard for her, digging up all the pain from the past. He should've thought of that before he ever went searching for Anna Coleson.

"I'm sorry, Mom."

"Sorry for what, Noah? You found that girl. You've protected her, kept her safe."

"Yeah, what Dad should've done all along."

She should've yelled at him, slapped him across the face, something for that comment.

Instead of the anger he deserved, she looked straight into his eyes with pity and sadness. "Is that why you went looking for her? Trying to undo your father's failures? Make up for what you think are his wrongs?"

"There were too many questions, Mom. I went out there for answers. Why did Sally run? She must know something. And why say 'what I think are his wrongs'? He had offshore accounts with payments from the gang responsible for killing a whole household! He was in on it! And by some fluke got caught in the blast. Yet we're the ones paying for it. We're the ones still feeling the repercussions."

Her eyes flashed.

There was the anger.

"I don't care how many accounts they find. Your father is innocent. He would never do what they accused him of." She stood up straight and tall and looked down at him. "You should be proud to have a father like Henry Dillard instead of stewing in your anger. Instead of changing your name like you're ashamed of him. He loved you. And I am convinced he died protecting the Colesons, not betraying them." She started to turn but stopped and looked back at him. "Where's your faith, Noah? God has not forsaken us. Your father's death doesn't change who God is. You'd best remember that."

She left, and her footsteps faded away. The locks on the front door clicked and the light in the living room went out as she passed through it.

Noah hung his head. Her question hung in the air. *Is that why you went looking for her? Trying to undo your father's failures?*

Was it?

It seemed like the answer to a prayer when the idea came to him. Watching Gregory's commercial brought back memories, memories of Nanny Carol's wild mustang stories, memories of four-year-old Anna and how much she loved the ranch and dreamed of helping the wild horses in the desert mountains. Something deep inside him knew he could find Anna. And while he didn't want a million dollars to spend on fancy cars or anything, they *were* on the verge of losing the ranch. Thus his quest for the truth about his dad and a way to save the ranch too.

He drove to San Jose and met with Gregory, promised him that he could find Anna and they struck a deal over Excalibur. All that confidence back then had almost dwindled away to nothing after seven months of searching when he caught sight of Carol dropping off that trailer at her neighbor's ranch.

But his mother's remark hit hard. True, there was always a sense of shame in being Henry Dillard's son that he was eager to shed. So, maybe deep down, he *was* trying to prove something. Trying to show the world that he was nothing like his father, a betrayer, by finding the family he swore to protect.

He looked at his father's forever empty chair at the head of the table.

Okay. Accused betrayer.

No one really knew the truth about what happened that night.

Except maybe Carol.

Was his mother right? Was his father set up to take the blame? Did he die a hero or a traitor?

Maybe Noah was just mad because either way, he died. Life insurance claims were denied because of the charges against his father. His mother couldn't make enough to stay in San Jose. He lost his dad, his friends, and his home. What kid wouldn't be bitter and at least a little lost after that?

But it wasn't just that.

The taunts. He could still hear them.

Noah Dillard
His daddy is a killer
He'll follow in his steps
And make a big mess
BOOM!

Friends one day turned and mocked him the next day with that chant over and over again. So many times that it got into his head. He couldn't help but wonder if they were right. Would he follow in such horrific steps? Was he bound by blood to the same fate?

So maybe this quest *was* to prove something.

His mother's voice asked again, *Where's your faith, Noah? God has not forsaken us.*

But it sure felt like it sometimes. Like it was all up to him to fix. His mother's cancer, paying the medical bills, keeping the ranch going. He was the only one left to bring some semblance of honor to this family, to look all those mockers in the eye and show them that he amounted to something. That he was a man of honor, not a traitor or a failure. That he was nothing like his father. Or at least that he wasn't like the man they portrayed in the papers.

His mother was right. If he sifted through all the memories, memories he had pushed back for so long, the man in the papers didn't look anything like the man in real life.

He was the kind of father that made Noah feel important. The kind of father that apologized when he blew his top. Noah watched his father care for his sick grandmother at the end of her life. He helped friends, served their neighbors, and was a good dad.

Nothing indicated that Henry Dillard was the kind

of man to work with gangsters to kill his family friends and employer.

Maybe he let the childish rhyme and media image overshadow all the other memories of his father.

Where's your faith, Noah? God has not forsaken us.

And maybe he was letting his troubles and burdens overshadow what he knew of his Heavenly Father too.

FIFTEEN

An obnoxious rooster crowed outside the window. Talia moaned and cracked an eye open. Dust motes danced in an early morning sun ray peeking through the slit between the two curtain panels. She might as well stop denying it. She was awake.

She burrowed deeper under the stack of cozy quilts. Soreness throughout her body demanded she stretch and move slowly. The last few days were taking a toll.

And where usually she was ready at any time to take a stand and fight for truth, she just wanted to get to Gregory and leave Noah to his happy life here. The life she had always wanted. A ranch, a loving family, a home. All she managed to bring the poor guy was a lot of pain and bodily harm. So before she was tempted to hope for more, she needed to leave.

She wiped a rogue tear that escaped and rolled down her cheek.

The rooster *cock-a-doodle-doo*'d once more. Fine. She sat up. The sooner she was up, the sooner she could get out of here.

After a shower, she changed into clothes that Marcy left for her, jeans and a Robin Valley High sweatshirt.

The jeans she said were Janey's, but she couldn't be sure about the sweatshirt. The sleeves hung past her fingertips. She'd rather attribute it to the baggy style of the times rather than think that she was wearing something soft and comfortable of Noah's.

She was a fool to think she could have a future with someone like Noah.

No matter who his father was.

He had no more control over that than she did at picking her family.

No. More than anything, she was upset because she let herself envision what life would be like with him. She thought they were connecting, but she knew better. She wasn't the kind of woman who did relationships. She needed to remember that and keep her guard up.

And they needed to leave as soon as possible so she wasn't tempted to forget it.

She followed her nose to the scent of coffee and pumpkin emanating from the kitchen, where she found three small children sitting at the dining room table. They stopped chattering and stared at her. A young woman with chestnut curls and the same eyes as Noah wiped sudsy wet hands on a dish towel and approached.

"Anna!"

She engulfed her in a hug. "I can't believe Noah found you. I mean, of course he did. You two always had this weird connection. But years of never knowing where you were, if you were safe, or what happened…and now you're here!"

She finally stepped away, and Talia tried to smile, but that knot of whatever it was inside was only growing bigger. Stronger. And what was she supposed to do with all that?

"Uh, you must be Janey?"

"Oh, yes. I'm sorry. You probably don't remember me. But, yeah, I'm Janey, Noah's sister. Wow, you look so much like your mom!"

"I… I do?"

Janey nodded. "Yeah. She was so beautiful. Alena and Ava took after your dad. But you have that light hair, the same high cheekbones of your mother." She stopped and, with a head tilt and pointer finger to her chin, studied her closer. "But your eyes are the same color that your dad's were."

That stupid knot grew bigger. A tension in her throat made it hard to swallow.

Janey didn't seem to notice.

"Come sit down, and I'll get you some coffee and muffins. Mom is out in the barns. Noah and my husband, Tom, are looking at the ranch truck, trying to decide if it can make it all the way to San Jose or not."

Hopefully it was reliable enough and they'd be back on the road soon.

Since bringing up eye color, Talia couldn't help but notice that three pairs of eyes, all varying shades of hazel and brown, stared at her as she took a seat at the table. Janey whirled through the kitchen, checking on something in the oven, refilling orange juice for the kids, and setting a mug of coffee in front of Talia.

Should she try talking to the miniature humans?

Noah came into the kitchen, and the little munchkins came alive with shouts of "Uncle Noah!" They rushed him and clamored for his attention.

"Hey, what are you goofballs doing here? Shouldn't you be in school?" He gave them a mock scowl as he leaned one of his crutches against the wall and scooped up the youngest in his arms.

The little girl with curls like her momma giggled. "Uncle Noah, I only go to pweschool."

The other two, boys, dragged a chair to Noah. The second his bottom hit the seat, one nephew proceeded to climb on his back and the other sat on his lap with his sister. "Yeah, and besides, it's Saturday."

Janey set a plate of hot pumpkin muffins on the table. "Boys, give your uncle a little space. You wild monkeys are going scare off Anna."

But Noah didn't seem bothered at all as he ruffled one boy's hair and kissed the little girl's cheek. "Nah, it's okay. I missed these guys. And Talia here is used to working with animals."

He sent her a wink. Again, she felt the wall inside slipping.

She had to get out of here now! She took a big gulp of hot coffee and burned her tongue. "Is the truck ready?"

Noah scratched his head and grimaced. "Not quite. Tom said he can fix it, but it will take a few hours."

"But I need to get to Gregory. Sally is still missing—"

"I know. But I called your uncle's office. He's out of the country right now. He'll be back on Monday, though. I've talked to Justin, too, and they're doing all they can to find Sally. He suggested staying here. Thought it would be safer. And the only thing we would be doing in San Jose is waiting in a hotel room all weekend for Gregory to return. Do you mind waiting until Monday? We can leave bright and early."

No, she didn't want to wait until Monday. She wanted to leave now.

But the little blond boy climbed off Noah's lap and

made himself at home on hers instead. "Pretty please, can you stay until Monday? I want to show Uncle Noah my costume, but it's not done yet. And I missed him."

He was a very serious-looking child. How could she deny those pleading eyes and take Noah away from his adoring niece and nephews? Especially when Gregory wasn't even in the country.

Noah spoke up too. "What do you say?"

Now five pairs of eyes stared at her. Waiting for her decision. This is what family looked like, and as much as it killed her to be with Noah any longer than she had to, reminding her of all she would never have with him, Janey and Marcy had already shared information about her family that whet her appetite. She was hungry for more. If she had to wait to see Gregory, maybe staying here another day or two would help fill that void. And there were plenty of ways she could avoid the temptation with the puppy dog brown eyes sitting next to her.

"That's fine. But I'd like to leave as soon as possible Monday."

The children cheered, and Janey grinned.

At least the decision made them happy. She just needed to guard her heart from falling for this family any more because when she left, she would probably never see them again.

Noah got his way. They were staying a couple more days at home. But it wasn't as relaxing as he thought it would be. The threat still hovered over them. He couldn't let his guard down. Talia depended on him.

The musty smell of the century-old barn mixed with his sweat. Excalibur, the black stallion, munched his oats, while Noah balanced on his good foot and used the pitchfork as a crutch to move to the next stall. The dumb surgical boot slowed him down. Usually he could muck all the stalls in half the time. Three more to go and then he could shower.

If only a shower could wash away more than the odor that clung to him.

Watching Talia with his family was eating him up inside. It was as if he was seeing what his life could've been if he weren't Henry Dillard's son. Even if his father wasn't guilty like his mother said, the world didn't think so. Noah lived with a stained name. A name that spoke of failure. Even though he tried to change it, change their family history by joining the marines, Noah's own failure in Afghanistan proved the blood in his veins was still Dillard. A name Talia could never want.

It almost seemed like she knew it too. She avoided him since they arrived last night. Maybe she was just anxious to meet Gregory and worried about Sally. Or maybe she came to her senses and realized he was someone whom she should stay away from.

The space wasn't a bad thing for him. It gave him time to get over her. Get used to living life without her again.

But even when he was on the other side of the ranch from her, he thought of her, remembered the sweet scent of her breath on his cheek when she kissed him at the cabin, the way she felt in his arms. But he knew better than to think he had a future with any woman.

He finished the last stall and then hobbled out to the path behind the barn. He should do a perimeter check before he took that shower. He might not be much of a protector, but he was all Talia had for now until he delivered her to her uncle. As much as he wanted Janey and Tom to stay at their own place and out of danger earlier today, they insisted on doing the opposite, claiming there was more protection if they stayed together. But now they were back home. Noah had their two ranch hands keeping an eye on things out toward the back of their property, but it was a lot of land for three men to watch over.

Noah used his crutches as he limped around the back of the ranch house and the barns. The fall evening was quiet. A couple coyotes howled but nothing else notable. No other signs of predators.

His body screamed for rest and another dose of meds to fight the pain, but he took the short trail through the woods right outside the barn.

Still nothing. Good. Noah stopped by the tall pine right at the edge of the forest and leaned his crutches against the trunk. He groaned as he slowly rotated his shoulders and arms, sore from the day's hard work and the extra burden of using the crutches. He leaned his body against the sturdy tree to rest a moment before heading inside and facing Talia. He should savor every second he had with her, because their time together was quickly coming to a close. Why was he out here in the woods?

Buck up, Landers, and finish the job.

As Noah pushed off to stand on his good foot, his elbow knocked one of the crutches to the ground. He grunted as he bent over to pick it up and then froze.

What was that? Something white on the ground.

A pile of cigarette butts, half-buried in pine needles. He kneeled down and studied them. Someone had been standing there for quite a while. Watching them.

He stood again and hurried back to the house. He

shouldn't have brought Talia here. He should've borrowed his mother's Jeep or something and found another way to get Talia to San Jose. Who was he kidding thinking he could keep her safe?

The ranch house was quiet with Janey and Tom and the kids gone for the night. Talia hummed as she searched the house for Noah, three ibuprofen tablets in one hand and a glass of water in the other. She ran into him as he walked through the front door.

"There you are. Your mom sent me to give you these." She dropped the pills in his hand without touching him, but when he went to take the glass, his fingers covered hers for a long second, and the sensation about knocked her to her knees.

"Talia, we need—"

"Take the painkillers, Noah."

He rolled his eyes but swallowed the pills. "Happy?"

Yes. More than she ever wanted to admit. She was happy here, and it terrified her. But a simple nod would do.

"We need to go. Now. Someone has been watching us."

"How do you know?"

"There's a pile of cigarettes at the edge of the woods. I don't like it."

"Maybe it was a bunch of teenagers."

"There? No. If they were going to hang out somewhere, they would find a better place. But from that spot, you have a clear view of the barnyard and the front of the house. I think whoever is after you found us." His breath whooshed out, and he took off his hat and slapped it against his thigh. The cloud of dust filled the space between them.

She wasn't ready to leave. She'd started to feel like a part of a family here, and she wasn't ready to be ripped away from it. And maybe it didn't make sense, but she felt closer than she ever had to her parents, her siblings, as Marcy and Janey shared stories over dinner. Even Noah's niece, little Darla, found her way onto her lap after the meal and helped her in a rousing game of Spoons while Noah was out in the barn. It felt like a home here. And she felt safe here.

Until now.

"You said my uncle wasn't even in the country. Where are we going to go?"

"I'm not exactly sure."

As much as she didn't want to lose the sensation she wanted most, to belong, she also couldn't stand the thought of any harm coming to Marcy and Janey's family. "Maybe we should stay here tonight and leave first thing tomorrow morning. Early. If we left now, we'd arrive in the middle of the night. Where would we stay? In your truck?"

"I don't know, Tal." Noah hopped to the couch and sat. He fiddled with his hat, turning it over and over in his hands. "That probably is the best we can do for now."

"Then what's the problem?"

"What if something happens to you?" He looked up at her, and his voice dropped. "I don't know what I would do."

She dropped down next to him and clasped his arm. "I believe in you, Noah. You've kept me alive this long. What's one more night?" A horrible thought took root, and she let go of him, leaving her cold. "Or…are you anxious to get rid of me?"

"No! It's not that. I, well, I don't think you should rely on me to keep you safe any longer than you have to. Look at what my dad did."

"You really think your dad killed my family?"

His face went pale. "I don't know."

"You said it was his honor to protect my family. How could he say that on the one hand and then work with a gang to murder them all?"

"It doesn't make sense, I know. My mom thinks he was framed. Set up somehow to take the blame."

"But what do you believe?"

He stared at the rug, a hollow tinniness to his voice. "I don't know. I mean, as a kid, he was my hero. There was no way he could do those things. But, well, basically my whole world fell apart. And I was angry. It started to chip away at this version of my dad I remembered. And then I lost someone I was close to, someone I was supposed to protect. When she died, all I could hear was the voices of my classmates chanting that I would be just like my dad and follow in his steps. Make a big mess. And I did."

So that was the grief he carried, the burden he blamed himself for. That was why he changed his last name. "Who was she?"

He didn't answer for a while. Just when she was about to ask again, he cleared his throat. "Kelley Donalds. She was a translator that worked with my platoon. I was assigned as her bodyguard as she tried to help with some humanitarian projects. But…" His voice trailed off.

"What happened to her?"

"We were walking into a dangerous territory, heard

there was a woman needing immediate medical attention. Kelley insisted on going to translate for our medics, but before we could get there, we were ambushed. I tried—" his voice caught "—I tried to cover her, but there was an explosion and a hail of gunfire. When the smoke cleared, she was…gone. And like my father, I failed. They were right. I followed in his steps."

"Noah, you were in a war zone. You're not responsible for that woman's death."

"Tell that to her family. I was her bodyguard. I'm alive. She isn't."

He looked up at her then, grief etched into every feature. For once the emotion on his face registered effortlessly.

He really thought it was his fault?

"What about all that stuff you were telling me in the car, about forgiveness?"

He scratched his head. "What about it?"

"Didn't you tell me that I should forgive Sally, let go of the pain and hurt of her lying to me and not hold it against her?"

"Yeah…"

She folded her arms and glared at him. "Well, when are you?"

"What are you talking about?"

"When are you going to forgive yourself?"

Noah bolted off the couch and hopped over to the fireplace, his strong arm holding him up as he leaned on the mantel. "Talia, that woman was killed because of me. How am I supposed to forgive myself for that?"

"The same way you told me to earlier. You take it to the One who forgave us. You don't need to keep carrying around the blame. As much as I need to learn to forgive, maybe you need to learn how to be forgiven."

The flames from the fire reflected in his eyes as he snapped his head up and practically growled. "What do you know?" His gaze shifted to the blaze once more. "I don't expect you to understand."

No, guess he wouldn't. Silly to think she was finally connecting to people, fitting in, belonging.

What *did* she know? She might wish to be the kind of woman who knew what he needed, who could connect with him. Help him. But she wasn't.

Before she became a puddle at his feet in some lame attempt to comfort the broken hero, she said good-night and slipped out of the room.

She turned out the lights and curled up in the dark on Janey's old bed. She didn't even take her boots off or brush her teeth. She lay in the dark, staring at the moon outside the window, wishing she was someone else. Someone normal.

Noah added log after log to the fire long after Talia said good-night until a tickle started in the back of his throat. He covered his barking cough with his arm and hobbled to the kitchen for water before he found something to punch or kick.

She didn't think he was to blame for Kelley's death? Who else was there? How could Talia, sweet, guileless, beautiful Talia, or anybody else understand how desperate he was to wash off the stain that covered and suffocated him?

"Still walking around with the weight of the world on your shoulders, son?"

He jumped and then flipped the light switch on the

stove, which illuminated his mother's slim form curled up in a chair at the breakfast nook. "Mom, what are you doing sitting here in the dark? Shouldn't you be in bed?"

"I was. But I thought I heard something and couldn't fall back asleep. I came out here to make some chamomile tea. Would you like some? Add a little honey and it might help that cough."

"No thanks." He plopped down and propped his crushed foot onto one of the other chairs.

She dunked her tea bag up and down in the steaming liquid. "So, what's keeping you up so late?"

Something in him searched in the darkness for hope. "Mom, do you really think Dad was framed? That he was innocent of everything they accused him of?"

She nodded. "Without a doubt. Your father was a good man. Not perfect by any means, believe me. I lived with him for fifteen years."

A memory flashed. "Remember how he used to lose his temper with the lawn mower, when it wouldn't start?"

Her laugh rang out. "Oh, he had such a hard time with that machine. It became such a point of frustration, and yet he wouldn't hire anybody else to mow the lawn." She smiled down at her mug. "He was never one to shirk his duty." Looking up, she laid a gentle hand on Noah. "Just like you. And just like you, he was an honorable man. A good man. So, I know. There's no way those accounts were his." A serious look crossed her face. "But there *was* an account I didn't know he had."

"Really?"

"The only funny thing about it was that it was here at the bank in town while we lived in San Jose. And there wasn't much in it. Just a few hundred dollars. Even though he never talked to me about it, he put my name on the account. He must've opened it that same week he died." She took a sip of tea. "I still have it. Your father nicknamed it the ICOE fund. I like to think it was one last way he was taking care of us."

"In Case of Emergency fund?"

She nodded.

"That sounds like him. At least, the part I remember."

"Noah, with all you remember of your father, how can you think he would be guilty of doing something like they've accused him of?"

He leaned back in his chair and scrubbed his face with his hands. "I don't know. All my friends hated me and said I would be just like him. Everywhere we went, people were slamming him, hating us for what happened. And then it wasn't even about truth as much as I just wanted to prove to everyone that I wasn't like that. I lost faith in him, I guess. Listened to all the speculation and blame."

"Sounds a bit like when we question the love of our Heavenly Father. It clouds our vision and gets in the way. We focus on trying to fix ourselves. Yet all along, His love for us isn't changed. It's steadfast. Faithful even when we are not."

"Yeah. I think I lost sight of that." And maybe if his father wasn't guilty, if he really was the man of honor he remembered, maybe Noah could be too. Maybe Talia was right, and he didn't need to hold on to the guilt of Kelley's death. Maybe it was time to forgive himself.

He spied a familiar ratty stuffed animal on a chair. "Sunny. How'd this get here?"

"I don't know. Darla came prancing through the kitchen with it. She claimed Anna gave it to her, but it needed surgery because the leg was falling off. I'm supposed to sew up the hole in the seam and give it back to her tomorrow."

Noah picked up the stuffed animal and found the hole. "Wow. Déjà vu. Instead of a four-year-old Anna Coleson dragging the poor horse around by the tail, it's four-year-old Darla."

"It's not just any horse. It's Mustang Sunny." She laughed. "I can't believe after everything you two have been through, that mustang survived!"

As Noah was about to set it back down on the table when he felt something weird, something hard within the stuffing. "What's this?" He poked his finger farther in the hole and touched a piece of metal. He worked it out until it clattered on the table. "A key?"

"Hmm. That looks like a key to a safety deposit box or lockbox of some sort. But why would it be in Talia's stuffed animal?" his mom asked.

"I don't know—wait. 'Key equals mustang'!"

"What do you mean?"

"Sally, or Carol, had written 'key equals mustang' on a notepad and had all of Talia's childhood toys out. We found Sunny at Talia's place. It's just a fluke we even had the horse when we escaped there."

His mother's voice dropped. She rested one of her hands on his arm. "Not a fluke, Noah."

A sense of reverence settled over them. Right. After all this stuffed animal went through, it couldn't be a coincidence that it was here now. "Alright, maybe by design. But why would Carol put a key in the stuffed animal and not say anything?"

"Maybe she's not the one who put it there." She looked out the window and then back again. "I'd love to talk with Carol about that night. I always wonder if she and Anna were the last ones to see Henry alive."

"You think so too?"

"How else would they have escaped the explosion? It was late at night. Anna should've been in bed like all the others. Maybe your father knew something was up and was able to warn them. He never took the night shift, but he told me he felt like he needed to that night. I think that he died trying to get to the rest of the family." A flash of grief passed through her eyes. She got up and put her mug in the sink. "You know, dear, I think I'm ready for bed. Will you be up for a while? You should get some sleep too."

"I'll turn in soon. Promise. But we're going to leave first thing tomorrow instead of waiting until Monday if you don't mind me taking your Jeep."

"Of course not. If you think it's best, take it. I'll see you in the morning." She kissed his head. "But promise me when everything is settled, you'll bring Anna back."

"Ma—"

"Noah, I see the way you look at her. Don't deny it."

Before he could respond, she left the kitchen and softly called over her shoulder, "Good night, son."

For the first time in a long time, the hope that sometimes sparked caught and grew. Maybe there was a chance. A chance Talia could see beyond his name, the accusations against his father, a chance she could see beyond his failures.

If there was, he needed to know. He hurried through the living room, as if the fragile spark would grow cold if he didn't see Talia now. Besides, he needed to tell her about the key.

The door to Janey's old room was cracked open,

moonlight streaming into the hall and cutting the darkness. A shadow flickered, and for a second the light disappeared.

A noise from inside the room urged Noah forward. He pushed the door farther. Inside his sister's old room, the curtains billowed and twisted in the wind. The window was open, screen popped out. But there was no sign of Talia anywhere.

SIXTEEN

Talia woke up shivering and sore, a frigid cement floor beneath her. Dark stale air surrounding her. Her tongue thick and bone-dry in her mouth. She started to sit up, but the floor tilted, and a pounding in her head had her fighting to keep the contents of her stomach down. She let out a groan.

"Talia, are you awake? Are you okay?"

"Sally?"

"Yes, it's me. Did they hurt you? Are you alright?"

Talia squinted, only able to see a shadowy figure. She'd never heard that panic in Sally's voice before. She lifted her hand to her head and felt a bump behind her ear and a sticky cut. She did a quick inventory of her arms and legs. They were achy from being curled up in a tight ball but fine. Her torso was sore, probably bruised, but nothing that would kill her. "I'm okay. Where are we?"

And how did she get here?

"I'm not sure. Some warehouse on the coast, I think. I saw it as we were landing, but then they blindfolded me until I was thrown in here. You sure you're okay? You've been out cold for a while now. What do you remember?"

"I have some bumps and bruises, but I'll be fine.

I don't remember much after going to bed at Landers Ranch."

"I think they drugged you." Sally scooched closer. "You were with the Dillards? They found you there?"

Talia sat up. Her vision cleared enough that she could see Sally next to her, hands bound in zip ties and ankles wrapped in duct tape. Talia started to rip away the tape with her unhindered hands. "Yeah, but I don't know how. At first, they were tracking us on our phones, but Noah was careful. Only his friend in the FBI and his mom knew where we were."

"But they've been watching Noah's family. I think that's how they found us in the first place. I heard them talking about having phones tapped and tracking devices. Pretty sure as soon as Noah found me, they knew where we were."

"Why are they tracking Noah?"

"Guess they knew he'd find us eventually."

"What do they want?"

"I don't know."

That wasn't going to fly anymore. Sally was alive and well. With that settled, all the other questions and accusations barreled through Talia's mind. "Really? You're still going to play this game, Sally? Or should I call you Carol? You don't need to lie to me anymore. I know the truth."

Sally scooted closer, grasping at Talia's sleeve. "Whatever you think you know, it's not everything, Talia. And I'm sorry I've kept things hidden from you. I did it to keep you safe."

Talia jerked her arm away. "You lied to me! You told me you were my aunt. You said everyone in our family died in a car accident. We were the only ones left. But that's not true."

"Tal—"

"I'm not done! You've kept me from my uncle for the last twenty-five years! You were just my nanny. We're not related. If it weren't for you, we probably wouldn't be in this mess!"

Sally's head jerked back as if hit. "What do you mean?"

"The Vasquez cartel. We know your family is somehow connected."

"You think that's what this is all about?"

"Isn't it?"

"I've lived all my adult life afraid it would come back to haunt me, that the sins of my father would follow me. But I don't think this is connected to the Vasquez family."

"Why not?"

"I don't think this is about a drug cartel or anything to do with my past. Because they're more interested in you than they are me." Her voice was just a whisper, but it caused a big quaking to start inside. Sally, with her wrists still bound grabbed her hand in a desperate squeeze. "I'm sorry, Talia, for not telling you everything. I only wanted to keep you safe. You have to believe me."

"Is that why we had to move so much? It wasn't just because I had such a hard time with kids in school?"

Sally shook her head. "Oh, sweetheart. I hated having to move you so much. Just when we would get settled, something would frighten me. A stranger following us or even too many questions from the school would make me wonder if they found us. I didn't even know who 'they' were. I couldn't risk it. So, we ran. The only thing that ever mattered to me was keeping you safe. After all your family did for me…it was the least I could do."

Talia looked from Sally's bruised and bloodied hands to her weathered tan face, also sporting deep purple bruises and a long scratch across her cheek. "What did my family do?"

"Your mother and grandparents are the ones that helped me escape my father and the Vasquezes. Papa was an accountant for the cartel. He was arranging my marriage to one of the sons. I was only fifteen. I ran away, and by God's grace your mother found me, took me in. She helped me get my visa, change my name and begin a new life in the US. She taught me English, and she helped my brother too. She offered to pay for college when the time came, but I was so happy just to be with your family, to help watch you and your brother and sisters. I know I'm just the nanny, but I've loved you all since the day you were born. And I would do anything to repay what your mother did for me. Losing them all that day—never knowing if it was my fault, if my father found me—it's a burden I bear daily. But with all that's happened in this last week, I think this is something else entirely."

"Was it Noah's father? Not sure what we did to make him hate us so much—especially when the rest of the family is so kind."

"Henry Dillard? He didn't hate your family. He saved us."

"Then why would he have helped the East Fourteeth Street gang? Where did those accounts come from?"

"I've never for a second believed those allegations. And maybe I should've come forward to clear his name, but for your sake, I couldn't. I had to keep you hidden and safe."

Dizziness struck again. Talia rubbed her temples as more questions flooded her mind. "If your family was from Venezuela, where did you get all those stories about the wild mustangs in the Owyhees?"

"When I was learning English, I had a pen pal from there. She would write beautiful stories about the horses. I always thought it would be an amazing place to live. And it is. I've loved every moment we've had together there, Talia."

"But now there's nothing left. The barn, the house, they burned down."

"What?"

Talia told her what happened at Mustang Sally Ranch. "Whoever is after us took everything."

Through her tears, Sally reached for her hands. "Not everything, cariña."

Talia looked around the bare floor, cold metal walls. Sure looked like they took it all. They were in an empty box.

The San Jose traffic might be the thing that pushed Noah to the brink of despair. The sun peeked over the hills to the east. The all-night drive was getting to him. Noah pounded the steering wheel of his mother's Jeep. His coffee tumbler rattled in the cup holder. Road rage. He finally got it. The endless line of vehicles in front of him stood in his way, and there was nothing he could do about it. And he was so close. But a Sunday morning traffic accident was seriously causing problems.

"Come on!" he yelled at no one in particular. He had

to get to Gregory. He was the only one who could help Talia and Sally now.

And if he never got the chance to tell Talia the truth, about how he felt about her— No, he couldn't go there. Couldn't think that way.

He had to find her. There was no other option.

"Move!"

The white van in front of him crawled a few more inches.

Lord, help me. I need to find her. I've made a mess of things. I've been blinded by anger for so long, trying to prove I'm different than what everyone said about my father. The truth is, I'm no better. But I know You forgive me. Please help me find her. Not because I deserve it, but because You are good.

The prayer born out of desperation brought peace even though traffic didn't move for the next twenty-eight minutes.

At last, the cars in front of him started a slow crawl forward. Soon the traffic unsnarled, and they were moving at the speed limit again.

Noah zipped through the streets until he came to the Coleson high-rise in downtown San Jose. He parked and rushed as fast as his crutches could carry him to the huge glass-and-steel structure. As a kid, he had loved coming here with his father. As they walked to the front door, their reflections would bounce off the bright windows. His dad would stick out his tongue and cross his eyes, making Noah laugh.

But there was nothing funny about coming here today.

He crossed the lobby and took the elevator to the top floor. For being a Sunday, there sure were a lot of people working. He waited while five others got off on different floors before the doors finally whooshed open for his.

Noah approached the receptionist outside of Gregory's office. "I need to speak to Gregory."

She didn't bother to look up from her computer screen. "I can make an appointment with Mr. Coleson. But the first available time won't be until next week. He's out of the country."

"No. I need to talk to him today."

A shadow passed by the frosted glass window behind the reception desk, drawing his attention.

The woman continued typing. "I'm sorry, but Mr. Coleson is not available."

"Who's in there now?" He pointed to the office door behind her.

She finally looked up at him. "That doesn't matter. I can make an appointment for you, or you can leave."

"You don't understand. People will die. I need to see Coleson. Right now!" He leaned over the desk toward her.

He had to be there. Who else would be in that office?

She stared him down without a flinch. The woman was not intimidated in the least.

Noah dropped his shoulders and sighed. "I just need to talk to the man. Please."

A beep sounded, and the woman touched the headpiece in her ear. Her lips thinned, but her voice was chirpy. "Right away, sir." She took off the headset and left without another word.

What?

The door behind her desk opened, and Gregory Coleson walked out. "Noah Dillard. No need to yell at Diane for following my instructions. Come in." He held the door, and Noah stepped in for the second time that year.

Still smelled the same. Like a rich coffee, leather and expensive cologne. The morning sun sparkled on the sleek glass-and-metal furnishings of the spacious corner office suite and glinted off Gregory's gold tie pin. The man looked like something from a business commercial. Power suit. Strong jawline. A serious smile meant to both intimidate and look like he cared. And it worked.

Hopefully the caring side would be evident today.

"Take a seat, Noah. I assume you have an update on Anna?"

As soon as Noah sat, his leg started bouncing, and his mouth went dry. Gregory walked to the window and looked out on the city as he took a sip from an expensive-looking mug.

"Uh, I do have an update. I... I found her."

Gregory's head whipped toward Noah. "Wonderful! Where is she?"

"Well, sir, that's why I'm here. I need your help."

"Of course. What do you need?"

"I...uh...lost her. No, I mean, I didn't lose her. She was taken. From my house. And I found the nanny first, Carol. But she was taken too. And so, I wondered if—"

The warm smile on Gregory's face disappeared. He marched up to Noah. Slammed the mug on the desk. "Let me get this straight. You had my niece, and the nanny, and now they're gone?"

"No, I. Yes. See, Sally was kidnapped a few days ago, and Talia, I mean, Anna was with me until just last night. I went to check on her and she was gone. Taken. The window was open, and footsteps outside show that someone was there. If I could—"

"Did you not sit there earlier this year and promise me that you could locate and protect my niece?"

"Yes, sir."

"In fact, I think your words were, 'I'm nothing like my father. I will find her and protect her with my life.'"

"I've been thinking. I'm not sure my father did anything wrong—"

"I don't care what you think. Your father killed my family. I had extreme doubts when you came here and said you had an idea to locate Anna. But I'm desperate to find her. And I thought, 'I shouldn't judge the son based on the father,' so I gave you a chance. And now you sit here and tell me that she was with you, and now she's gone again?"

"Yes—"

"Then what you are saying is that you are exactly like your father, Noah Dillard. You failed to protect her. And if anything happens to her, it is on you." He pointed toward the door. "Leave."

Noah stood. "Please, Mr. Coleson, Anna means so much to me. If you could just help—I don't know—I'm sure you have some resources, someone to help me track down these people. I just want to find her."

"Let me make this very clear. I never want to see your face, or any other Dillard, ever again! Enough Colesons have died because of your family. Get. Out."

There was nothing else to do.

Noah left.

Talia closed her eyes and leaned her head against the metal wall. She might not be able to discern a lot of social cues and people's motives, but deep down she knew Sally loved her like an aunt, or maybe even a mother.

Sally chose this life, to take care of Talia like she was her own. She left any family she had to be Talia's family.

Maybe Noah was right when he said that's the kind of family that mattered. And it was time to forgive her.

But her blood family. That still mattered too. Talia needed to know the truth. She looked over at Sally sitting next to her. "I just don't understand why you would keep me from my own uncle."

"Talia, the only people I knew I could trust died in that explosion."

"What happened that night? How did we escape?"

A sad smile appeared on Sally's face. "You are the reason we escaped."

"Me?"

"You fell asleep on my lap earlier that evening, and I carried you to bed and tucked you in. Later you woke up crying for your mustang and wouldn't go back to sleep without Sunny. So, while everyone else slept, we searched the house. Out on the back patio by the pool, we found Henry. I think he picked up the stuffed animal somewhere on his rounds. He also had my Bible and was handing it back to me. At that moment the first bomb went off. He looked at me and said, 'The key is in the mustang. Now run. And no matter what, don't trust anybody, Carol. I mean it. Nobody! Just keep her safe!' He ran straight toward the house and shouted for me to tell his family that he loved them. As he went inside the back door, more bombs went off. And so I did what he said. I took you and ran."

"How did the police know the East Fourteenth Street gang were involved?"

"The papers said the police received a tip that they supplied the bombs. I think they found bomb-making supplies or something. They found the money trail leading back to Henry Dillard, but I never believed it. His horror and shock were too real. But I do think he knew something about who was behind it all."

"The key is inside the mustang? What was he talking about?"

"I don't know. It was only when I saw Noah that I even remembered Henry saying those words as we ran. I thought he meant for me to take his car. The Mustang. But now I wonder if he was talking about something else."

"I wish we had a key now, something to get us out of this place." Talia went to the door. It was made of some kind of metal. Too heavy to crash or kick down. The lock on the other side must be solid since the door wouldn't budge. She gave it a pound with her fist and started pacing the room. Twelve paces one way. Turn. Then twenty paces more. "I want to meet my uncle. And… I need to see Noah."

"If he's anything like his father, he won't stop until he finds you."

Yes, he had that hero quality in spades. But what would happen after he found them? Being torn from his presence had a way of waking her up to what really mattered and what she wanted. She might not be able to connect with everybody, but she knew him. She was comfortable with him.

"Talia, how do you feel about him?"

"You know I hate that question." She marched again and counted on her fingers. "I won't tell you what I feel, but I'll tell you what I know. Noah took a bullet for me. He was almost killed trying to save our animals. He treats me like I matter. He looks at me like I'm already beautiful without changing a thing. And when he does…" She stopped and pictured his face, and her voice dropped to a whisper. "I have the strongest desire to kiss him like it is the most natural thing in the world. Like it's instinct."

"Don't look now, dear, but I think you might love him."

"Maybe, but we won't know unless we get out of here and find Gregory. He can help us find the truth to clear Henry's name."

"I've been here for two days and haven't found any way out of this room. I think it's an empty storage facility in a warehouse or factory. There's a bathroom almost too disgusting to use and that's it. My kidnappers came twice yesterday to leave me food and a bottle of water and once to throw you in here."

"And they haven't been back since?"

She shook her head.

They walked over to the heavy metal door again. Talia laid her ear against it but couldn't hear anything. "Let's see if there's anything in the bathroom we can use to cut that zip tie around your wrists and bust out of here."

"I'm warning you, it's not for the faint of heart."

"I work with animals. How bad can it be?"

She opened the door to the putrid closet-like bathroom.

It was bad.

She pulled her shirt up over her nose and held her breath. Just a rusty sink and disgusting toilet. But there was a small cloudy mirror over the sink with a thin metal frame screwed directly into the wall.

Talia took one of her cowgirl boots off. "Stand back."

"What are you doing?"

"Following Noah's advice. Improvising." She used the heel of the boot to smash the mirror. She ripped the tail of her shirt to wrap around one of the biggest shards of glass and used it like a knife to cut the zip tie around Sally's wrists. "Now we just need to find a way out."

SEVENTEEN

Noah hobbled out of the fancy high-rise to the fountain in front of the building. The sunlight reflected off the water feature, the glare killing his eyes. He turned his back to it and sank down to the bench-like ledge. His crutches clattered to the ground.

He'd failed.

He'd lost Talia. He couldn't even save Sally's barn.

That look of disgust on Gregory's face was deserved. He promised to find his niece and keep her safe. Because of him, the woman he loved was in danger. He couldn't blame Gregory for kicking him out of his office.

His phone buzzed in his pocket. Had it been anyone else, he would've ignored it. He swiped to answer. "Hey, Mom."

"Did you make it to San Jose?"

"Yeah. But Gregory wants nothing to do with us. He won't help me. I don't know where to go from here."

"Noah, you don't have anything to prove to Gregory Coleson. But if you love Anna, you won't give up until you find her."

"Mom, are you hearing me? I'm out of options. I failed to keep her safe."

"She might be out of your hands, but she's still in God's. And so are you. This isn't the end, Noah. You found her once. You can find her again."

"I know I started on this mission as a way to prove something, but honestly, right now I just want her safe." Safe and in his arms. The being in his arms part was a long shot. But he needed to try.

"I know. You love her, don't you."

"I've known her for four days, Mom."

"It can still be the beginning of love. And it's been more than four days. You've known her since she was born."

True. He smiled at the memories of Anna as a baby and toddler and a bossy preschooler demanding he get down on his knees and let her clamber up on his back. Anna as a grown woman hadn't changed too much. Give her a horse, boss him around, and she was happy.

And he'd give her everything he had to make her happy. But he had to find her first. He picked his crutches up off the sidewalk and stood. "I've got to find her. I'm going to give Sheriff Daniels and Justin a call and see if they know anything. Did you find out about that key?"

"Oh, yes! I forgot why I called you in the first place. Remember that savings account? The one Dad opened here in Robin Valley? When I called and asked about safety deposit boxes in general, they said they do have one on record in our name. It was free with the savings and checking account he opened. I know it's a long shot, but I'm going there to see if this key you left me fits. Janey will be here any minute to take me."

"Good. Maybe there will be something valuable we can sell to save the ranch once Gregory rescinds his offer for Excalibur and makes us pay him back everything he's already given us. And be careful. Someone broke into our house. They might be watching still."

"The police were here but found nothing. They think whoever took Anna is long gone."

"Maybe. Just be cautious."

"I will. I'm proud of you, Noah. Now go get our girl."

Noah hung up, trying to swallow past the lump in his throat.

Lord, you helped me find Talia once. Please keep her safe and lead me to her again.

He made it to his mother's car and called Sheriff Daniels.

"Sorry, son. We passed everything we had to the FBI agents who came and took over the case. Smart call on using those agriculture drones to track down the vehicles, though. Might have to work with Dr. Stanton on other cases. But as far as the Knowles lady, we were told to step down from the investigation."

Noah thanked him and called Justin next. "Please tell me you got something. Coleson was a dead end. No help at all."

"I might. But I'm still running down some leads. Why don't you come to the office, and by the time you get here, I'll know some more?"

Thirty minutes later, Justin led Noah through a maze of cubicles and offices. "It was a nightmare trying to trace Carol Force's background. But with the information you and Anna gave us, we were able to track down a brother in Seattle. From the looks of it, he escaped the cartel life too. He's married. Has a couple of grown kids and no ties to Venezuela or the Vasquezes that we can find."

"So it was a dead end."

"Looks like it. But we got more off the guys at the Nampa Airport. These two thugs are definitely part of the East Fourteenth Street gang. The FBI office up in Salt Lake City that helped us with that sting tracked down the threats Talia was receiving. Led back to Dwight Quincy. But I can't find any connection between him and the street gang."

"This goes back to the original explosion that took out the rest of the Coleson family?"

"It's gotta be."

"Why are they after Talia after all these years?"

"I don't know, dude. Someone has a serious vendetta against this family. If there is any connection to the Vasquez cartel, I can believe Sebastian Vasquez is nasty enough to go to this length to kill every member of a family, but I don't know why. I've opened up the cold case, and I'm going back to threats against the Coleson Company from twenty-five years ago. I'm coming up with nothing."

"Is it because the Colesons helped Carol escape the cartel?"

"That's the only thing I've come up with too, but I can't find a single piece of evidence to support that."

Noah slumped in his chair. Why else would anyone want to kill Anna Coleson? His phone beeped again. "Yeah, Mom?"

"Noah." Her voice sounded strange. "I know who took Anna."

A way out. Talia said it like it was no big deal. But after a thorough inspection of the walls and floors of the twenty-four-by-forty-foot room, she came to a conclusion. The only way out was the thick metal door. No windows to crawl through. No walls they could break through. No vents or air ducts either. Nothing. A lone fluorescent light hanging from the tall ceiling, too far out of reach to be useful, was the only fixture in the room.

Sally threw down the pointed end of the zip tie she was using to try to pick the lock. "It's worthless. We're stuck."

"Well, if we can't open the door ourselves, we'll just have to wait for them to open it for us."

"And they're just going to let us waltz out of here?"

"No. We'll have a surprise waiting for them." Talia stalked off to the restroom and held her breath again before entering. Her boots crunched on the broken glass from the mirror as she hefted the slab of porcelain that covered the tank of the toilet. She carried it to the door and set it carefully on the floor. "We'll wait here. As soon as we hear anybody coming, I'll grab this and knock whoever opens the door upside the head, and we can escape."

"Then what?"

"We'll find Gregory and Noah."

Sally nodded. "About that… Talia, I'm sorry I didn't tell you about your family, about your uncle. And I'm sorry for telling you I was your aunt. I didn't know who to trust. It was you and me against the world. I thought I was doing the right thing. But you're right. I should've told you the truth."

"Did you think I couldn't handle it?"

"At first. But you've shown me that you can. I think part of me started believing the lie, that you were my niece, and I hated the thought of losing that connection, losing you."

Talia dropped her gaze to her boot tips. "I've been

so caught up in my own struggles that I never stopped to think about yours. What it must've been like to leave your own family, your country, to take a four-year-old girl on the run and keep her safe, raise her all alone. And for a long time, you were right. I couldn't handle anything changing my controlled little world."

"And now?"

She looked up to see the one person that had been with her through everything. That sacrificed for her sake. No matter what the title or blood work said, she was family. "I'm learning to branch out a little more. Improvise."

The sound of footsteps outside the door brought the conversation to a halt. Talia grabbed the makeshift weapon and stood beside the door. Her arms started to shake with the weight lifted high over her head.

The knob jiggled. The door creaked open, and a bald man stepped in. Talia hurled the lid down on his shiny head as hard as she could. He crumpled to the floor.

It worked!

Quietly they scrambled over him and out into an open warehouse filled with crates and boxes stacked on industrial shelves and pallets. Talia led Sally to a tower of boxes. They hid behind it while Talia scoped the room for an exit. There was an empty skid loader, but it was useless without the keys. The windows were too tall to use. They would have to skirt around the outside wall and find a door. The good news was that nobody else seemed to be around except the man they took down.

"We should go while the coast is clear," she whispered to Sally.

They rushed to the aisle of wooden crates, ducking for cover and jogging along the row until they reached the end. They crossed a wide break and then ran along another row. There! A door. They would have to cross a large open area, but a red exit sign glowed over the top of the door. They'd found a way out.

Shouts from behind them startled Talia. They must've found their guy. Sally poked her and pointed to the door. "We have to run for it."

"We'll be exposed."

"They're coming. It's now or never."

She was right. Footsteps running toward them accompanied the shouts. They dashed out from behind the last crate and onto the open floor. Almost there. Her heart pounded. Closer.

The door opened. Talia skidded to a stop. Sally froze.

The silhouette of a man in a suit filled the doorway. Bright sunlight behind him cast his face in the shadows. Their exit was blocked. They were spotted.

No!

A breath caught in Talia's lungs, burning for release.

The man stepped toward them. The door slammed shut. Without the sunlight, his face came into focus.

Wait. She knew this man.

Strong jaw, piercing blue eyes. Light brown hair streaked with gray.

The breath Talia had been holding released. She rushed to him. "Uncle Gregory!"

They were safe. Finally.

"Anna? Is that you?"

"Yes, please, you have to help us. These men kidnapped us."

Sally didn't move any closer. She glanced behind them and then back to the door.

Gregory studied Talia but said nothing.

Maybe he didn't believe she was really his niece. Noah did say there were impostors over the years, pretending to be her.

"You have to believe me. I'm Anna. I'm the one you've been looking for."

Why wasn't he doing something?

"Anna Coleson?"

"Yes! See, and there's Sally. I mean Carol. Nanny Carol. She's been keeping me safe all these years. But these men are trying to kill us. Please help. We have to get out of here." She grabbed his arm and started toward the door. "Is Noah here? He must've found you for you to be here."

Gregory was still looking at her with a strange expression on his face. "It really is you, isn't it?"

"Yes, that's what I've been trying to tell you. But we have to leave now. We can catch up later." Another tug on his arm. But he didn't budge.

Instead, he grasped her wrist and squeezed. "Now, now. Why would I let you escape when I went through all this trouble and expense to bring you here?"

EIGHTEEN

Noah put the call on speaker. "Mom, what did you find? Who has Talia?"

"I couldn't believe it. It was there. In the box."

"Mom! Who has Anna?"

"Your dad, he tried t—" Her voice broke.

Noah clenched his jaw tight. Justin leaned closer to phone. "Mrs. Landers, this is Justin Miller. I'm with the FBI, and any information you have would be really helpful. Did you find something?"

"It's Dillard. Marcy Dillard, and yes, I found something. Proof that Gregory Coleson had his family murdered."

"Gregory? Mom, what are you talking about?" It didn't make any sense. How could it be the man willing to pay a million dollars to have his niece back? "Are you sure?"

"Yes. Your father had a copy of Doug and Colleen's will, photos of Gregory meeting with some men that I think might be from the East Fourteenth Street gang, financial statements, and notes. Lots of notes. I skimmed them, and it seems like Henry and Doug found Gregory making business deals for navigation tech with questionable clients. People they thought were associated with terrorist groups. They were trying to gather more evidence before turning it over to the authorities when they died."

"But why would Gregory want the whole family dead? Why is he looking for Talia?"

"Because she's about to turn thirty."

"What does that have to do with anything?"

"It looks like Gregory had a lot of debt and ended up selling most of his shares of the company to Doug. And according to the will, everything, including those shares of the Coleson Company, went to Colleen. If Colleen died, everything was put into a trust for the children with certain stipulations. If the inheritance wasn't claimed by the time Anna turned thirty years of age, then everything would be turned over to various charity groups, and the US military would get rights to all technology and company shares."

"He killed them all for the money?"

"Yes, upon proof of death of all the heirs *before* Anna's thirtieth birthday, from what I understand, everything would've gone to the next of kin. That must be Gregory."

Justin spoke up. "Right, but there was no proof of death for Anna Coleson."

All the pieces began to click in place. No wonder the desperate search for her. He needed a dead body to gain access to the Coleson fortune before it slipped out of his greedy hands.

Justin gave Marcy instructions on what to do with the evidence she found. Noah's mind could only focus on one thing though. As soon as Justin ended the call, he asked, "Where does Coleson have her? She wasn't in his office. I was just there."

"That's a huge building. He could've kept her anywhere."

"Yeah, but we're talking about a guy who has others do his dirty work. The street gang doing the bombing. Framing my dad. He won't want to keep her anywhere associated with him. And all he needs is her dead body. We have to find her now!"

They pulled up a map, and Justin was on the phone again with Organized Crime. "I need the most recent info you've got on the East Fourteenth Street gang, local hangouts, businesses, properties, anything." Justin stormed out of the office and out into an open area. "I need anyone who is able to help me now!" He gave them a rundown, and they divided the list of known locations and names. "We're looking for a place the East Fourteenth Street gang could be hiding her. It's probably something local since Coleson is here. Might be close to an airport or landing strip since we know a private jet is involved. Hop to it. This woman's life is on the line."

It seemed like forever before someone yelled, "Got something!"

Noah hopped over on one foot to the woman's desk.

She pointed to a building on the map on her computer screen. "Here. The owner of this warehouse is a known associate of the head of the gang. They think this shipping station is how they're transporting the drugs. It's close to a private air strip."

Noah pounded the desk. "That's gotta be it."

Justin studied the screen a little longer. "It's our best guess. Everything else is too public. I'll get a team together and roll. If we find a better target, we'll reroute."

Noah blocked Justin's path with his crutch. "I'm coming with you."

"Landers, you're injured. Wait here and I'll go get her. Trust me."

"It's Dillard, actually. And it's not that I don't trust you. I need to see this through. I have to find her."

Justin rolled his eyes and started marching away. "Fine. I know you're too stubborn to stay. Might as well keep you close so I can watch your back. But you better keep up."

Soon they were suited up in Kevlar and on their way to meet a SWAT team near the site. Once there, Noah stuck to Justin's side as he coordinated with the SWAT leader. The building, a shipping warehouse near the south end of the bay, wouldn't be easy to breach. One exit and multiple loading docks in the back, and two doors in the front, with massive space in between to try to cover. They had no idea how many people would be inside or what kind of layout they were walking into.

One of the agents ran up and interrupted the coordination efforts. "Justin, Nguyen ran plates on the vehicles in the parking lot. One is registered to Coleson."

"Good work. That's the confirmation we need." Justin directed the others, then turned to Noah. "I know you want to be in on the action, but you should stay out here."

"You can't bench me now. I'll be fine."

"How are you going to do this with crutches?"

"I'll stay behind you and watch your back. It's either that or I go in alone and look for Talia."

A grunt sounded enough like a "fine" for Noah to follow as Justin jogged to the corner of the building. A voice over the coms counted down. At *one*, their team rammed the door open, and agents streamed in, guns raised. Justin and Noah entered last. The others spread out like a line of ants. The wall of agents moved through the room. With hand signals, they cleared the space and started moving toward the aisles of crates and boxes.

Chaos erupted as men in street clothes swarmed the aisles and started firing. Shots reverberated off the metal walls.

Justin and Noah ducked behind a crate. A few feet away was a reach truck, a pallet with a tall stack of boxes already loaded on it. Noah tapped Justin on the shoulder and pointed. Noah slipped into the cab and started the machine. He moved forward toward the men in the aisle in front of them. Justin used the cover of the boxes and took down the enemy in their path. The other SWAT members found cover too and continued to fire.

A blast threw Noah from the truck.

Justin sprawled on the floor. The gunshots stopped as the smoke overtook them. Grenades?

Noah coughed, crawled to Justin. His eyes were closed, body still.

"Justin, come on, man."

The smoke aggravated his lungs, and the cough wracked Noah's body.

Justin opened his eyes. Moved slowly to sit up. "Told ya you should've stayed back." His voice was weak, but he was alive. They couldn't see the other agents in the smoke.

Justin called for a head count. Static on the coms. Finally, a few voices came through.

After a quick count, it sounded like they were down three men. Justin rose to a squat, staying behind the boxes. "Okay, now they've really ticked me off. Team, let's get these scumbags." He turned to Noah, who couldn't stop coughing. "I need you to stay here and watch that door we came through. You'll give away our position with that cough, so move to the end of this aisle and keep your butt there. Cover the exit."

What about Talia? He had to find her. Another cough wracked his body. He couldn't stop long enough to breathe. The damage from the smoke inhalation was too much.

And he couldn't risk anybody else's life. He would have to trust the rest to find her.

He pushed Justin toward the fight he so desperately wanted to join while the coughing overtook him. His lungs spasmed. He sat against the reach truck and fought to breathe.

Lord, help keep her safe.

Talia still couldn't fathom it. The man on the television, the eyes begging for help to find her, the voice imploring the public for any information leading to her, had morphed into this cruel monster dragging her through the warehouse with a gun pointed at Sally.

They were back in that bare room, the stench from the bathroom overpowering. How could they be back here?

Another man burst into the room. "Coleson, you brought the feds in on us. This was not part of our deal!"

Gregory let out a string of curses and yanked Talia close. "This is all your fault, you little brat! You should've died with the rest of them!" He looked at the other man. "Kim, you better find a way out of here or we're all going down."

"Why don't you just kill them now, and we can run for it?"

"No, at this point they'll be our hostages. If we have to, we can negotiate our escape."

Kim grabbed Sally and pushed her through the door, back to the open warehouse. Gregory followed.

An enormous boom sounded. Talia's knees buckled under her.

"Oh, no you don't." Gregory jerked her back up and dragged her.

Kim led them between the furthest row of containers and the outer wall. "This way leads straight to the door. They've got the loading docks under fire, but I had my men clear a path for us. They're holding them off, but not for much longer. Let's go!"

The aisle in front of them filled with smoke. Coughs and gunshots seemed to be coming from every direction, paralyzing Talia. She collapsed to the cold floor.

"Get up!" Gregory wrenched her arm.

She tried but couldn't. Panic seized her body.

He got back down in her face. "If you don't get up right now, you will see your precious nanny die." He pointed a gun at Sally and released the safety with a deafening click.

No! Somehow, she found the strength to stand again, and they advanced right into the smoke. She could barely see Sally's barn jacket in front of them. Gregory's vise-like grip on her arm was cutting off circulation. But the fog in her head was clearing.

This man wanted her dead.

If she didn't escape now, she would join the rest of her family.

She wasn't ready for that.

She wanted her own family. With Noah. Sally. She didn't want to go down this way.

Talia dragged her feet, resisting Gregory. She had to slow them down. They were reaching the end of the aisle now, close to the wide-open area. Just beyond that would be the door.

"Move!" Those icy blue eyes bore into her. "Or die."

"You're going to kill me anyway. Why should I make it easy for you? You killed my family. You burned down our ranch, our home. Why?"

Kim and Sally disappeared in the smoke.

A growl sounded from Gregory's throat. "I don't have time for this. Kim!" He dragged her forward.

A thump of something heavy hitting the floor came from in front of them.

"Kim?"

The smoke grew thicker. Someone was coughing. Talia's eyes watered.

Gregory took a tentative step forward. Then another. He started to call for Kim again, but he was cut off with a cough. She pulled back, but the distraction didn't weaken his hold on her arm. Another step forward.

Out of the thick gray haze, something metal glinted high. A rod?

Whatever it was swooped down and crashed into Coleson. A shout and scuffle freed Talia. She shot forward and bumped into Sally. Kim lay unconscious at her feet. Sally held a gun steady, pointed at the floor but ready to take a shot as she watched two men wrestle in the aisle of the warehouse. A familiar crutch leaned against a box, and another slid across the cement floor as it was kicked away in the skirmish.

Noah!

Sure enough, his handsome face emerged as the smoke started to clear, Gregory subdued beneath him.

He coughed and wrenched Gregory up to standing. He spoke into a communication device. "Justin, I got them." He shoved Gregory toward Sally. "Sally, you got this?" His voice wheezed.

She pointed the gun at Gregory's chest. "Yes, I do."

"Good, because I have something I need to do." He fastened Gregory's hands with a zip tie from his vest pocket and then snatched his one crutch at his feet.

His dark chestnut eyes locked on to her. He hopped over, and she knew exactly what he wanted. She was so ready. He wrapped his arms around her and pulled her close. Pressed his lips to hers, lips that were full, soft. She couldn't get enough of the minty sweetness of his kiss. A heady mixture of passion and desire.

Kissing him was the most natural and exhilarating experience. Her curiosity was satisfied, and yet she hungered for more.

Noah.

When he pulled back slightly, he rested his forehead on hers. "I know you want facts, so I have one for you. I love you."

He had proven his words were true. He showed her in multiple ways he cared about her.

She spent enough time trapped and locked up in an empty room to know what it would feel like to push him away. It wasn't the life she wanted.

"Yes, I believe you."

His eyes closed, and he smiled. "Good," he whispered. He opened his eyes once more. "I would love to spend the rest of our lives showing you what true family is if you'll let me. What do you say?"

She answered him with a kiss of her own. For once she knew exactly what the emotion was welling up inside. Love. But it was more than just a feeling. It was a choice. A decision. And Noah was the person she wanted to love for the rest of her life. She wasn't going to let him go anytime soon.

EPILOGUE

A pair of spring robins flitted in the tree outside the Landers Ranch porch. The male added another twig to their nest and flew off. Noah watched the female rearrange his twig and add a bit of fluff of her own as he downed the last of his coffee.

The slap of the screen door alerted him to his mother's presence.

She sipped from her own mug. "You ready?"

"More than ready. You'll meet us there?"

"Wouldn't miss it for the world. Tell Anna I'll be there shortly. I'm riding with Janey."

Noah waved goodbye as he hopped into his old red Ford. He cruised down Clover Road into town and parked next to the feed store. His cowboy boots thumping on the sidewalk, he passed the store entrance and opened the front door of the next building. The smell of new paint and a strong cleanser made him cough.

Sally slapped him on the back as he stepped into the lobby. "Still got those weak lungs, Noah. Buck up. Can't have your coughing mess up our big day."

"Yeah, yeah. Is my wife ready?"

She laughed. "You like calling her that, don't you?"

"Still can't believe it most days."

"It's only been three weeks since the wedding."

Anna marched into the room and started pacing. "You two at it again?"

Noah grabbed her hand and pulled his wife into his arms. "Yeah, that's what families do. Bicker." He kissed her lightly on the lips. "And speaking of family, Mom will be here soon. Janey and Tom and their crew are on the way. What can I do to help?"

"I need you to help calm these nerves."

"I can do that." He went in for a kiss.

Sally snorted. "Hey, honeymoon's over, you two. We have a business to open and a ribbon-cutting ceremony in an hour. Get to work."

Noah lost himself in Anna's laugh. The worry lines in her brows disappeared. Her blue-eyed gaze landed on the glass front door. She tugged his arm and led him outside, and they stared at it together. "It looks good, huh?"

He wrapped an arm around her and kissed her temple. "It's perfect."

Coleson-Dillard Equestrian Care and Mustang Rescue.

"You two ready for all this?" A deep voice behind them chuckled.

Noah spun around to see Justin Miller walking toward them, taking off his sunglasses. "Hey, you're early."

"As much as I appreciate the invite, I can't stay for the ribbon-cutting. My time in San Jose is up. I came to give you an update in person before I head back to Montana."

"What's up?"

"The Coleson case is officially closed. Since the gang leader, Kim, turned on Gregory and gave us everything we needed months ago, it was a clear-cut case. Just took a while to tie up all the loose ends, but here we are." Justin took in the new signage on the door. "So running Coleson Company wasn't enough of a job for ya?"

Noah pulled Anna in closer to his side. "We don't want to live in the city, so we'll stay here and do the work we love. When Anna needs to, she's close enough to drive down to San Jose and do whatever needs to be done with her family's company. She has some good board members and staff working for her."

Justin nodded slowly, a hint of envy and maybe a little heartbreak lingering in his eyes. "Looks like you've got it made, man." He held out a fist.

Noah bumped it with his own. "Yeah, but semper fi, bro. If you ever need anything. I'm here for you."

Anna spoke up. "*We're* here for you. Thank you for helping us." Instead of holding out a hand like she normally did, she actually moved in to give Justin a light hug. Looked like the Dillards were rubbing off on her.

"Thanks for that. Keep my boy in line, Talia." Justin stepped back.

"It's Anna now. Anna Dillard," she said with pride.

Noah looked down at her cute smirk as they all laughed. He had to admit, Anna Dillard had a nice ring to it. Before long, they might be picking out more Dillard names as their own family grew.

And hopefully he would be as good of a dad as Henry Dillard was.

* * * * *

Dear Reader,

I hope you enjoyed reading *Hidden Ranch Peril*. For a few years, my husband and I lived in Idaho. For entertainment, we would often pack up the kids and go for drives. The Owyhee Mountains were one of our favorite places to explore. We always hoped to spot wild horses, and sometimes we did!

The sagebrush-covered hills of the Owyhees, though, are rather desolate in many places. It's the perfect place to hide and not be found. But where there are creeks or springs, where there is water, you will find trees. Life.

Noah and Talia may have felt alone in the world, desolate. But in searching for truth, they find each other, and more importantly, they come to the Living Water and find forgiveness and life. I pray you will too.

In His abundant grace,
Michelle Aleckson

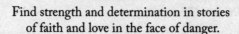

COMING NEXT MONTH FROM
Love Inspired Suspense

TRACKING A KILLER
Rocky Mountain K-9 Unit • by Elizabeth Goddard
The last thing K-9 officer Harlow Zane expected when she and cadaver dog Nell join an investigation is to draw the killer's obsessive attention. But FBI special agent Wes Grey notices she matches the victim profile, and when another look-alike goes missing, they must work together to catch the criminal...before Harlow's the next to disappear.

HIDING IN PLAIN SIGHT
by Laura Scott
Fleeing to her uncle's home is Shauna McKay's only option after her mother's brutally murdered and the murderer's sights set on her. Local sheriff Liam Harland's convinced hiding Shauna in an Amish community will shield her—until an Amish woman who looks like Shauna is attacked. It's clear nobody in this peaceful community is safe...

FUGITIVE AMBUSH
Range River Bounty Hunters • by Jenna Night
While pursuing a dangerous bail jumper, bounty hunter Hayley Ryan barely escapes an attack by the fugitive. Teaming up with rival Jack Colter results in the discovery of another criminal—one who's been missing for years. Can their uneasy partnership—and lives—survive their search for not one but two notorious escaped felons?

ROCKY MOUNTAIN VENDETTA
by Jane M. Choate
With her husband's killer released from prison and dead set on revenge, former US marshal Brianna Thomas's fake identity's no longer enough to protect her and her little girl. Now snowbound in the Rockies with the only person she can trust, ex-marshal Gideon Stratham, she must survive a storm *and* the convict's vengeance.

TWIN MURDER MIX-UP
Deputies of Anderson County • by Sami A. Abrams
After capturing a murder on camera, photographer Amy Baker becomes the next target—and her identical twin is killed instead. Now on the run with her sister's newborn, Amy turns to Detective Keith Young, her childhood crush. But when they discover Keith is the baby's father, can he regain Amy's trust...before the killer strikes again?

ESCAPE ROUTE
by Tanya Stowe
While flying above the Texas border, helicopter pilot Tara Jean "TJ" Baskins witnesses a ruthless murder. Now a deadly gang wants her out of the way. Border patrol officer Trace Leyton—her old friend and the man who once betrayed her—is determined to catch the ring's leader...until the search leads to Trace's family.

LOOK FOR THESE AND OTHER LOVE INSPIRED BOOKS WHEREVER BOOKS ARE SOLD, INCLUDING MOST BOOKSTORES, SUPERMARKETS, DISCOUNT STORES AND DRUGSTORES.

LISCNM0722

Get 4 FREE REWARDS!

We'll send you 2 FREE Books plus 2 FREE Mystery Gifts.

FREE Value Over $20

Both the **Love Inspired®** and **Love Inspired® Suspense** series feature compelling novels filled with inspirational romance, faith, forgiveness, and hope.

YES! Please send me 2 FREE novels from the Love Inspired or Love Inspired Suspense series and my 2 FREE gifts (gifts are worth about $10 retail). After receiving them, if I don't wish to receive any more books, I can return the shipping statement marked "cancel." If I don't cancel, I will receive 6 brand-new Love Inspired Larger-Print books or Love Inspired Suspense Larger-Print books every month and be billed just $5.99 each in the U.S. or $6.24 each in Canada. That is a savings of at least 17% off the cover price. It's quite a bargain! Shipping and handling is just 50¢ per book in the U.S. and $1.25 per book in Canada.* I understand that accepting the 2 free books and gifts places me under no obligation to buy anything. I can always return a shipment and cancel at any time. The free books and gifts are mine to keep no matter what I decide.

Choose one:
☐ **Love Inspired Larger-Print**
(122/322 IDN GNWC)

☐ **Love Inspired Suspense Larger-Print**
(107/307 IDN GNWN)

Name (please print)

Address   Apt. #

City   State/Province   Zip/Postal Code

Email: Please check this box ☐ if you would like to receive newsletters and promotional emails from Harlequin Enterprises ULC and its affiliates. You can unsubscribe anytime.

Mail to the Harlequin Reader Service:
IN U.S.A.: P.O. Box 1341, Buffalo, NY 14240-8531
IN CANADA: P.O. Box 603, Fort Erie, Ontario L2A 5X3

Want to try 2 free books from another series? Call 1-800-873-8635 or visit www.ReaderService.com.

Fleeing to her uncle's home is Shauna McKay's only option after her mother's brutally murdered and the murderer's sights set on her. Local sheriff Liam Harland's convinced hiding Shauna in an Amish community will shield her. But it's clear nobody in this peaceful community is safe...

Read on for a sneak preview of
Hiding in Plain Sight *by Laura Scott,*
available September 2022 from Love Inspired Suspense!

Someone was shooting at them!

Liam hit the gas and Shauna braced herself for the worst. Her body began to shake uncontrollably as the SUV sped up and jerked from side to side as Liam attempted to escape.

They were shooting at her this time. Not just attempting to run her off the road.

These people, whoever they were, wanted her *dead*.

Just like her mother.

Why? She couldn't seem to grasp why she'd suddenly become a target. It just didn't make any sense. Tears pricked her eyes, but she held them back.

After what seemed like eons but was likely only fifteen minutes, the vehicle slowed to a normal rate of speed.

"Are you okay?" Liam asked tersely.

She hesitantly lifted her head, scanning the area. "I— Yes. You?"

"Fine. Thankfully the shooter missed us. I wish I knew exactly where the gunfire came from." He sounded frustrated. "This is my fault. I knew you were in danger, but I didn't expect anyone to fire at us in broad daylight."

"At me." Her voice was soft but firm. "Not you, Liam. This is all about me."

He glanced sharply at her. "They could have easily shot me, too, Shauna. Thankfully, they missed, but that was too close. And you still don't know why these people have come after you?" He hesitated, then added, "Or why they killed your mother?"

"No." She shrugged helplessly. "I'm not lying. There is no reason I can come up with that would cause this sort of action. No one hated either of us this much."

"Revenge?" He divided his attention between her and the road. She didn't recognize the highway they were on, but then again, she didn't know much of anything about Green Lake.

Other than she'd brought danger to the quaint tourist town.

Don't miss
Hiding in Plain Sight *by Laura Scott,*
available September 2022 wherever
Love Inspired Suspense books and ebooks are sold.

LoveInspired.com

LOVE INSPIRED

Stories to uplift and inspire

Fall in love with Love Inspired—
inspirational and uplifting stories of faith
and hope. Find strength and comfort in
the bonds of friendship and community.
Revel in the warmth of possibility and the
promise of new beginnings.

Sign up for the Love Inspired newsletter
at **LoveInspired.com** to be the first
to find out about upcoming titles,
special promotions and exclusive content.

CONNECT WITH US AT:

Facebook.com/LoveInspiredBooks

Twitter.com/LoveInspiredBks